James Harry Pence

The magazine and the drama; an index

James Harry Pence

The magazine and the drama; an index

ISBN/EAN: 9783337306076

Printed in Europe, USA, Canada, Australia, Japan

Cover: Foto ©Andreas Hilbeck / pixelio.de

More available books at **www.hansebooks.com**

THE
MAGAZINE AND THE DRAMA

An Index

COMPILED BY

JAMES HARRY PENCE

"HAPPY SHALL I BE TO GIVE YOU THE INFOR-
MATION YOU DESIRE, IF YOU WILL USE YOUR
KNOWLEDGE IN SOME USEFUL WAY."
THE CHANCE UTTERANCE OF A FRIEND.

NEW-YORK
THE DUNLAP SOCIETY
1896

PREFACE.

I hate explanations. To me the crudest pencil-sketch means more than volumes of discussion, and I should like to feel assured that the following pages need no long commentary to make clear their excuse for existence. In them I have tried to give a convenient guide to the mass of literature the magazines have published concerning the acted drama and the men and women directly connected with it. Like the city directory, this guide gives no information in the concrete, but tells how and where that information may be found, — also, by whom it is given, and, in many cases, when it was issued. Such, in the main, is the scope of the present publication.

There are, however, a few features of the work that justify particular notice, as, for instance, the arrangement of matter according to writers as well as subjects. In this age, when the names of writers often count for nearly as much as what is written, circumstances can easily be conceived in which it may be of value to know what, on this subject, any particular writer, actor, or manager has said. This system also discloses the fact that many good men have had a good word to say for the drama.

It has been necessary to limit the scope thus outlined to articles on the acted drama; that is, that portion of the drama that has or has had a stage history. Magazine farces and stories in which the scenes or characters are theatrical but fictional, excellent as these may be, do not come within the limit, nor do the bright, interesting "Dramatic Departments" of the minor magazines and daily and weekly papers.

Dealing, as the present work does, with a special topic, it has been possible to divide the individual subjects more minutely and exactly than could be done in a general index, yet I should be ungrateful and insincere not to acknowledge my indebtedness to — I am almost willing to say dependence upon — the "Poole" and the "Fletcher" Indexes to Periodical Literature, one of the most valuable series of books this century has produced.

It is with pleasure that I acknowledge the courtesy of the late Dr. Poole's family, of Mr. William I. Fletcher, of Messrs. Houghton, Mifflin & Co., and of Mr. R. R. Bowker, in consenting to the adoption in this work of the lines and methods pursued in "Poole's Index."

Cincinnati, December, 1896.

Abbreviations.

Ag ....*August.*
Ap ....*April.*
D.............*December.*
F ....*February.*
Ja ....*January.*
Je. ....*June.*
Jl..................*July.*

My................*May.*
Mr.......,.......*March.*
N.............*November.*
n. s..........*New Series.*
O...............*October.*
S. ....*September.*
Same art....*Same Article.*

Acad.............*Academy* ....*London.*
Acad. (Syr.) .....*Academy* .... $\big\{$ *Syracuse, N. Y.;* *Boston.*
All the Year .....*All the Year Round.*.........*London.*
Amer. ....*American*.................*Philadelphia.*
Am. Bibliop.....*American Bibliopolist*........*New York.*
Am. J. Soc. Sci. $\big\{$ *American Journal of Social Science* $\big\}$ *New York.*
Am. Natural.....*American Naturalist.*........*Philadelphia.*
Amer. Q........*American Quarterly Review.*..*Philadelphia.*
Am. Whig R.....*American Whig Review* .....*New York.*
Anal. M........*Analectic Magazine.*.........*Philadelphia.*
And. R.........*Andover Review* ....*Boston.*
Ann. Register....*Annual Register.*............*London.*
Antiq...........*Antiquary* ....*London.*
Appleton ....*Appleton's Journal.*..........*New York.*
Arena ....*Arena* ....*Boston.*
Argosy ....*Argosy* ....*London.*

ix

Abbreviations.

Art. J......	....*Art Journal*	*London.*
Ath..............	*Atheneum*...................	*London.*
Atlan............	*Atlantic Monthly*...........	*Boston.*
Author...........	*Author*	*Boston.*
Bay State Mo. ...	*Bay State Monthly*	*Boston.*
Belgra............	*Belgravia*...................	*London.*
Bentley	*Bentley's Miscellany'*........	*London.*
Bibliog.	*Bibliographer*	*London.*
Blackw	*Blackwood's Magazine*	*Edinburgh.*
Brit. Quar. R	*British Quarterly Review*	*London.*
Broadw..........	*Broadway*	*New York.*
Cal. Ill........	{ *California Illustrated Maga-*	{ *San Francisco and*
	zine...................	*New York.* }
Canad. M	*Canadian Magazine*.........	*Toronto.*
Canad. Mo......	*Canadian Monthly*..........	*Toronto.*
Cath. World.....	*Catholic World*.............	*New York.*
Cent	*Century Magazine*...........	*New York.*
Cent. o. s........	*Scribner's Monthly*..........	*New York.*
Chamb. J........	*Chambers' Journal*	*Edinburgh.*
Chap-Book	*Chap-Book*	*Chicago.*
Chaut...........	*Chautauquan*................	*New York.*
Ch. R........	{ *Church Review, formerly*	{ *New Haven and New*
	American Church Review. }	*York.* }
Colburn	*Colburn's Magazine*	*London.*
Contemp.	*Contemporary Review*	*London.*
Contin. Mo......	*Continental Monthly*........	*New York.*
Cornh	*Cornhill Magazine*	*London.*
Cosmopolis......	*Cosmopolis*.................	*London.*
Cosmop	*Cosmopolitan*................	*New York.*
Critic...........	*Critic*.....................	*New York.*
Dark Blue.......	*Dark Blue*..................	*London.*
Dem. R.........	*Democratic Review*	*New York.*
Dial (Ch.)	*Dial*.......................	*Chicago.*
Dr. Mirror.......	*Dramatic Mirror*............	*New York.*
Dub. R.	*Dublin Review*	*London.*
Dub. Univ.......	*Dublin University Magazine*..	*Dublin and London.*
Ecl. M.	*Eclectic Magazine*...........	*New York.*
Ed. R.	*Edinburgh Review*	*Edinburgh.*
Educa...........	*Education*	*Boston.*
English Dom. M.	*English Domestic Magazine* ..	*London.*

Lond. Quart. R. . *London Quarterly Review* . . . . *London.*
Lond. Soc. . . . . *London Society* . . . . *London.*
Longman . . . . *Longman's Magazine* . . . . . . *London.*
Looker On . . . . . *Looker On* . . . . *New York.*
Luth. Q. . . . . *Lutheran Quarterly* . . . . *Gettysburg.*
M. Am. Hist. . . . . *Magazine of American History.* *New York.*
McClure . . . . *McClure's Magazine* . . . . *New York.*
Macmil. . . . . *Macmillan's Magazine* . . . . . . *London.*
Manch. G. . . . . . . *Manchester Guardian* . . . . . . { *Manchester, England.*
Manhat. . . . . *Manhattan* . . . . *New York.*
Meth. R. . . . . *Methodist Quarterly Review* . . *New York.*
Metrop. . . . . *Metropolitan* . . . . *New York.*
Mod. R. . . . . *Modern Review* . . . . *London.*
Month. . . . . *Month* . . . . *London.*
Mo. Rel. M. . . . . . *Monthly Religious Magazine.* *Boston.*
Munsey. . . . . *Munsey's Magazine* . . . . *New York.*
Murray. . . . . *Murray's Magazine* . . . . *London.*
Mus . . . . { *Museum of Foreign Literature, Littell's* . . . . } *Philadelphia.*
Nation. . . . . *Nation* . . . . *New York.*
National . . . . *National Review* . . . . *London.*
Nat. Q. . . . . *National Quarterly Review* . . . *New York.*
New Bohemian . . *New Bohemian* . . . . *Cincinnati.*
New Q. . . . . *New Quarterly Review* . . . . *London.*
New R. . . . . *New Review* . . . . *London.*
N. Eng. M. . . . . . . *New England Magazine* . . . . . *Boston.*
Nickell . . . . *Nickell Magazine* . . . . *Boston.*
19th Cent. . . . . . . *Nineteenth Century* . . . . *London.*
No. Am. . . . . *North American Review* . . . . *New York.*
No. Brit. . . . . *North British Review* . . . . *London.*
O. and N. . . . . . . *Old and New* . . . . *Boston.*
Once a Week. . . . *Once a Week* . . . . *London.*
Overland'. . . . . . . *Overland Monthly* . . . . *San Francisco, Cal.*
Pamph. . . . . *Pamphleteer* . . . . *London*
Penn Mo. . . . . . . *Penn Monthly* . . . . *Philadelphia.*
Peop. J. . . . . *People's Journal* . . . . *London.*
Peterson. . . . . . . { *Peterson's Ladies' National Magazine* . . . . } *Philadelphia.*
Philistine . . . . *Philistine* . . . . *East Aurora, N. Y.*

Poet Lore........	*Poet Lore*..................	*Boston.*
Pop. Sci. Mo.....	*Popular Science Monthly*.....	*New York.*
Portf	*Portfolio*....................	*London.*
Portf. (Den)......	*Portfolio (Dennie's)*	*Philadelphia.*
Potter Am. Mo...	*Potter's American Monthly* ...	*Philadelphia.*
Princ	*Princeton Review*............	*New York.*
Pub. Opin	*Public Opinion*	*New York.*
Putnam.........	*Putnam's Monthly Magazine.*	*New York.*
Quart	*Quarterly Review*............	*London.*
Radical.........	*Radical*	*Boston.*
Retros..........	*Retrospective Review*........	*London.*
R. of Rs.	*Review of Reviews*	*New York.*
Roy. Hist. Soc.	{ *Royal Historical Society, London* .... }	*London.*
St. James'	*St. James' Magazine*.........	*London.*
St. Paul's........	*St. Paul's Magazine*	*London.*
Sat. R..........	*Saturday Review*............	*London.*
Scand...........	*Scandinavia*	*Chicago.*
Scrib.	*Scribner's Magazine*.........	*New York.*
Select J.........	*Select Journal*..............	*Boston.*
Sem.	*Seminary*...................	*New York.*
Sharpe	*Sharpe's London Magazine* ...	*London.*
So. Lit. J.......	*Southern Literary Journal* ...	*Charleston.*
So. Lit..Mess....	*Southern Literary Messenger.*	*Richmond, Va.*
So. M..........	*Southern Magazine*..........	*Baltimore.*
So. R..........	*Southern Review*............	*Charleston, S. C.*
Spec............	*Spectator*	*London.*
S...............	*Sunday Magazine*	*London.*
Tait............	*Tait's Edinburgh Magazine.*	*Edinburgh.*
Temp. Bar	*Temple Bar*................	*London.*
The.	*Theatre*	*London.*
Tinsley.........	*Tinsley's Magazine*..........	*London.*
To-Day	*To-Day*	*London.*
Unit. R.........	*Unitarian Review*..........	*Boston.*
Univ. R.........	*Universalist Review*........	*Boston.*
Victoria	*Victoria Magazine*..........	*London.*
Wes. J..........	*Western Literary Journal*....	*Cincinnati.*
Western.........	*Western*...................	*St. Louis.*
Westm..........	*Westminster*	*London.*
Writer	*Writer*	*Boston.*

NEW-YORK·

FOUNDED IN

MDCCCLXXXV

THE DUNLAP SOCIETY

Matter contained in the index is arranged according to writers as well as subjects, and the names of writers are inclosed within parentheses. Thus, articles about Joseph Jefferson may be found under heading **Jefferson, Joseph;** articles by him under **(Jefferson, Joseph.)**

The Magazine and the Drama.

Abbott, Maggie Mitchell. *See "Maggie Mitchell."*

(Abbott, Wm.) Gossip of a Player. Knick. 24: 266, 359, 531 (S., O. & D.'44); 25: 14, 496 (Ja. & Je.'45); 26: 110 (Ag.'45).

(a Beckett, Arthur W.) Gilbert a Becket as a Dramatist. The. n. s. 9: 146.

> "Comedy of Errors" at Gray's Inn. The. n. s. 27: 31 (Ja.'96).

> Earnings of Playwrights and Players. The. n. s. 26: 209 (O.'95).

> "Faded Flowers": History of a Single-Act Play. The. n. s. 25: 204 (Ap.'95).

> Green-Room Recollections of Fechter. The. n. s. 24: 116 (S.'94).

> A First-Night Audience at the "Lyceum." The. n. s. 25: 68 (F.'95).

> Playing before Royalty. The. n. s. 24: 226 (N.'94).

> Is Stage "Realism" Outdone? The. n. s. 28: 132 (S.'96).

a Becket, Gilbert, as a Dramatist. (A. W. a Beckett) The. n. s. 9: 146.

Abington, Mrs. Fanny Barton. Colburn 52: 217.

> as Lady Teazle. (D. Cook) Gent. M. n. s. 16: 198 (F.'76).

I

(**Achorn**, A. C.)　Ibsen at Home.　N. Eng. M. n. s. 13: 337
(F.'96).

Acting.　Atlan. 68: 858 (D.'91).　Westm. 119: 190 (Ja.'83).
(H. Irving) Eng. Illust. 2: 643.　Same, Critic 6: 162.
Nation 37: 188 (Ag.30,'83).　(D. Cook) The.'82, 2:
140.　The. n. s. 25: 317 (Je.'95).
Amateur.　*See "Amateur," "Amateurism,"* etc.
Anatomy of.　(W. Archer) Longm. 11: 266, 375, 498
(Ja., F. & Mr.'88).
and Actors.　(C. Coquelin) Harper 74: 891 (My.'87).
and Authors.　(C. Coquelin) Harper 76: 679 (Ap.'88).
and Scenery.　Sat. R. 71: 549 (My. 9,'91).
as a Fine Art.　(H. Bamflyde) The. n. s. 12: 129.
as a Means of Making Money.　Sat. R. 69: 165 (F. 8,'90).
at the Comédie Française.　The. n. s. 22: 73 (Ag.'93).
Boucicault on.　Spec. 55: 987 (Jl. 29,'82).
Can it be Taught ?　(H. Aïdé) 19th Cent. 34: 452 (S.'93).
Concerning.　(R. Mansfield) No. Am. 159: 337 (S.'94).
Diderot's Paradox of.　*See "Emotionalism,"* etc.
Emotional, in Paris.　(K. Venning) The. n. s. 10: 240.
Hamlet on.　(P. Fitzgerald) The.'80, 2: 152.
in Earnest.　*See "Emotionalism."*
Irving on.　(" Ouida ") 19th Cent. 37: 786 (My. '95).
Murdoch on.　Sat. R. 56: 172 (Ag. 11,'83).
The Old, and the New.　(G. B. Shaw) Sat. R. 80: 799
(D.14,'95).
The Profession of.　The. n. s. 25: 255 (My.'95).
Psychology of.　(W. Archer) Ath.'89, 1 : 156 (F. 2,'89).
Some Views of.　(T. Salvini) Cent. 19: 194 (D.'90).
Study of, in Paris.　(J. M. Everts) Cent. 6: 471 (Jl.'84).
Talma on.　Sat. R. 55: 542 (Apr. 28.'83).　Nation 37: 188
(Ag. 30,'83).
Training for, Value of.　(W. Archer) National 7: 770.

Actor, The.　(John Drew) Scrib. 15: 32 (Ja.'94).
the Manager, and the Public.　(J. Malone) Forum 20:
235 (O.'95).

Actor, and his Duty to his Time. (W. Winter) The. n. s. 14 : 134.

He Would be an. (D. Cook) The.'79, 1 : 21.

Legal Status of. (T. Marricott) The. n. s. 25 : 260 (My. '95).

Life of an. (W. B. Kingston) The.'85, 2 : 183.

London, Forty Years' Recollections of a. (A. V. Campbell) Bentley 27 : 481 (1850) 28 : 156 (1850).

Obloquy of an. Knick. 6 : 216, 541 (S. & D.'35).

Management. *See " Management."*

Profession of. The.'85, 1 : 15.

Shakspere as an. (A. Cargill) Scribner 9 : 613 (My.'91).

Social Status of the. (J. Coleman) National 5 : 20 (Mr. '85). (E. Yates) Temp. Bar 8 : 183 (My.'63). Harper 78 : 316 (Ja.'89). (H. Aïdé) 19th Cent. 17 : 521 (Mr.'85). Sat. R. 59 : 8 (Je. 3,'85). In England (P. Fitzgerald) ; in France (F. Hawkins) ; in Germany (C. Lowe) The. n. s. 26 : 6 (Jl.'95).

vs. Author. Gent. M. n. s. 47 : 536 (N.'91).

Actors. Am. Whig R. 6 : 519 (N.'47). Blackw. 8 : 508 (F. '21). Knick. 18 : 207 (S.'41). So. Lit. Mess. 5 : 17 (Ja. '39).

Amateur. *See " Amateur."*

American. *See " American Actors,"* etc.

and Actors' Fund. Harper 79 : 474 (Ag.'89).

and Actresses in Westminster Abbey. Cornh. 67 : 373 (Ap.'93).

" Actors and Actresses," Matthews' and Hutton's. *See "Matthews," " Hutton,"* etc.

and Managers under Queen Anne. (G. A. Aitken) Ath. '88, 2 : 203, 267.

and their Salaries. Harper 2 : 403 (F.'51).

and Theatricals. Mus. 3 : 257 (S.'23).

Anecdotes of. Fraser 24 : 179 (Ag.'41).

at Drury Lane. Temp. Bar 16 : 540 (Mr.'66).

Blunders of. (W. Baynham) The.'79, 2 : 147.

Actors, Old, Studies of. Dub. Univ. 62 : 450 (O.'63).

Our. (O. B. Bunce) Galaxy 5 : 165 (F.'68).

Puritans and. (W. Wheater) Gent. M. n. s. 5 : 178 (F.'93).

Religion of. (C. Lamb) Colburn 6 : 405. Cornh. 15 : 429 (Ap. '67).

Reminiscences of. (J. F. Kirk) Lippinc. 33 : 604.

Salaries of. (J. Hollingshead) The. '79, 1 : 107. (A. W. a Beckett) The. n. s. 26 : 209 (O.'96).

Social Position of. *See "Actor, Social Status of," etc.*

Spanish. *See "Spanish Actors," etc.*

Strange. (D. Cook) Belgra. 45 : 51. Same Art. Appleton 26 : 267.

Strolling. Cornh. 72 : 87 (Jl.'95). Same Art. Ecl. M. 125 : 374 (S.'95).

Thespians out of the Cart. Tinsley 1 : 36.

a Word to. (R. K. Hervey) The. n. s. 10 : 133.

Young, Hints to. The. n. s. 18 : 72.

Actors, Old. Records of a Stage Veteran. Colburn 41 : 454.

Actors' Association. (W. Lestocq) The. n. s. 24 : 298 (D.'94).

Holiday. (M. Lemon) Ev. Sat. 4 : 747.

Memories. (W. E. McCann) Lippinc. 3 : 262 (Mr.'69).

Actress and " Actress." The. n. s. 28 : 59 (Ag.'96).

as Usurper of Man's Prerogative. Gent. M. n. s. (Ja.'96).

Strolling, Experiences of a. Chamb. J. 56 : 473.

Actresses, Famous. Appleton 20 : 158.

Recollections of. (M. E. W. Sherwood) Lippinc. 53 : 92 (Ja.'94).

Titled. (W. Bacheller) Munsey 13 : 46 (Ap.'95). (Mrs. Mathews) Bentley 17 : 594; 18 : 54, 601.

Who have become Peeresses. (A. C. Wheeler) Cosmopol. 20 : 130 (D.'95).

a Word About. Lippinc. 23 : 126 (Ja.'79). *See also "Women," etc.*

of the Age. (W. D. Adams) The. n. s. 22 : 67 (Ag. '93).

(**Addis**, J.) Jaques and the Duke. *See "As You Like It."*
Advertisement, Self-, the Art of. The. n. s. 28: 140
(S.'96).
Advertisement, Theatrical Curiosities of. The. n. s. 16:
221.

Adelphi and Haymarket, A Night at. Sharpe 41: 99.

"**Adrienne Lecouvreur.**" *See "Eugène Scribe."*

Æschylus. "Agamemnon." *See " College Theatricals,"* etc.

Age, the Comédiennes of the. (W. D. Adams) The. n. s.
22: 196 (O.'93).

Aidé, Hamilton. Victoria 34: 164.
Acting, Can it be Taught? 19th Cent. 34: 452 (S.'93).
The Actor's Calling. 19th Cent. 17: 521 (Mr.'85).
A Dramatic School. The. '82, 1: 73.
A School of Dramatic Art. 19th Cent. 11: 567 (Ap.'82).

(**Aitken**, G. A.) Theatrical Lawsuits. Head. 36: 135, 168.
Actors and Managers under Queen Anne. The. '88, 2:
203, 267.

(**Alberti**, C.) Writings of Gustav Freytag. National 10: 80.

(**Aldrich**, Mildred.) Alex. Salvini. Arena 7: 129 (Ja.'93).
E. H. Sothern. Arena 6: 517 (O.'92).
Juliets of the Stage. Nickell 6: 348 (D. '96).

(**Aldrich**, T. B.) Sargent's Portrait of Edwin Booth at "The
Players." Harper 82: 489 (F.'91).

Alexander, Geo., as Bassanio. The. '85, 1: 175, 203.
and Mrs. Campbell, portrait. The. n. s. 22: 92 (Ag.'93).
and Herbert Waring, portrait. The. n. s. 24: 29 (Jl.'94).

(**Alger**, W. R.) Friendships in Shakspere. Chr. Exam. 73:
209, 403.

Alisov, Mme. Harper 24: 270 (Ja.'62).

(**Allen**, G. W.) Mary Dyke Duff. Amer. 4: 170.

Allison, Wm.) Jane Hading. The. n. s. 22: 63 (Ag.'93).

(**Almy,** Percival H. W.)   New View of Oscar Wilde.   The.
n. s. 23: 119 (Mr.'94).

Amateur Acting.   (W. G. Elliott) National 24: 628.
Actor, An.   (D. Cook) The.'78, 2: 117.
Actors. Amateur-Professional. Sat. R. 69: 196 (F.15,'90).
Actors. Professional-Amateur. Sat. R. 69: 13 (Ja. 4,'90).
(T. E. Pemberton) The. n. s. 25: 17 (Ja.'95).
Actors.   All the Year Round 55: 282.   Sat. R. 55: 594
(My. 12,'83); 60: 806.
Actors, Hints to: Making-up.   Chamb. J. 64: 711.
Actors, Notes on.   Once a Week 13: 202, 232.
Actors' Club, Our.   (H. Souther) Tinsley 31: 83.
Actors in Camp.   (G. W. Watson) N. Ecl. 7: 513.
Actors in Ireland.   (M. E. Smith) Tinsley 32: 315.
Theatricals. Dub. Univ. 93: 474. Lippinc. 25: 515 (Apr.
'80). Bentley 3: 83. Colburn 83: 340. (G. Kobbé)
Cent. 15: 749.

Amateurs, About.   The. n. s. 23: 339 (Je.'93).   *See also*
" Private Theatricals," etc.

Amelia, Princess of Saxony, Dramas of. (C. C. Felton). No.
Am. 52: 487.

American, The, On the Stage.   (J. B. Matthews) Scrib. 28:
321 (Jl.'79).
The, on the English Stage.   (H. James, Jr.) Atlan. 68:
846 (D.'91).

American Actors in England.   Dem. R. 19: 186.   (W. J.
Lawrence) Gent. M. n. s. 46: 82 (Ja.'91).
Actors and Actresses of New York.   (J. B. Matthews)
Scrib. 17: 769 (Ap.'79).
Actresses (A. de Bremont).   The. n. s. 9: 324.
Actresses, Introduction of, on English Stage.   (W. H.
Hudson) The. n. s. 10: 255.
American Burlesque. (L. Hutton) Harper 81: 59 (Je.'90).
Comedy.   Harper 81: 152 (Je.'90).
Conservatoire, Shall we have an ? (F. H. Sargent) Cent.
6: 475 (Jl.'84).

American Drama. Harper 73: 314 (Jl.'86); 79: 314 (Jl.'89). (H. Garland) Lit. W. (Bost.) 20: 307 (S. 14,'89). (A. Daly) No. Am. 142: 485. (L. Hutton) Lippinc. 37: 289 (Mr. '86). (A. E. Lancaster) Potter Am. Mo. 8: 23, 346. (E. A. Poe) Am. Whig. R. 3: 117. Am. Q, 1: 331. Dem. R. 45: 554. Dub. Univ. 74: 319. Same art. Ecl. M. 5: 555. Lond. Mo. 16: 466.

Drama, Beginnings of. (R. Davey) National 19: 802 (Ag.'92).

Drama, Characteristics of (A. Hennequin) Arena 1: 700.

Drama, Future of. (D. Boucicault) Arena 2: 641.

Drama, Irving's Influence on. The. n. s. 27: 75 (F.'96).

Dramatic Literature, Beginnings of. (P. L. Ford) N. Eng. M. n. s. 9: 673 (F.'94).

Tours, Some. (T. Beaugeard) The. n. s. 26: 89 (Ag.'95).

Dramatic Outlook. (J. B. Matthews) 78: 924 (My.'89).

Dramatists. (A. Hornblow) Munsey 12: 159 (N.'94).

Dramatists, Shall We Have? (W. H. Page) Amer. 6: 169.

Stage. Harper 73: 477 (Ag.'86). (W. Archer) National 6: 401.

Stage, Beauties on. (J. P. Reed; W. S. Walsh) Cosmopolitan 14: 294 (Ja.'93).

Stage, Retrospection of. (J. Bernard) Manhat. 3: 604.

Theater. Am. Arch. 6: 20, 74; 35: 28 (Ja. 9,'92). (O. Logan) Galaxy 5: 22.

Theatre, Bernard on. Dial (Ch.) 7: 271.

Theatre, Dunlap's History of. Am. Q. 12: 509. Mo. R. 130: 151.

Theatre Endowed. (F. J. Carpenter) Dial 21: (O. 1,'96). (H. Modjeska) Forum 14: 337 (N.'92).

Theatre, the First. (G. H. Moore) M. Am. Hist. 21: 58.

Theatre, Seilheimer's History of. Ath.'90, 1: 156.

Americans at the Theatres. Ev. Sat. 10: 451.

"**Among the Gods.**" *See* "*Gallery*," *etc.*

(**Anderson,** D. J.) Harlequin *in extremis*. The.'79, 1: 103.

2

Anderson, Mary. The. 84, 1 : 52. (W. Archer) The.'85, 2 : 175.

Acting of. Sat. R. 58 : 343, 590.

and her Art. (W. D. Adams) The. n. s. 27 : 273 (My. '96).

as She is To-Day. (E. W. Bok) L. H. J. (Mr.'96).

Decline of. Critic 7 : 193.

in England, The.'83, 1, 321. (F. Wedmore) Acad. 24 : 168. (W. H. Pollock) Cent. 6 : 315 (Je. '84).

in " Ingomar." The.'83, 2 : 199.

in " Lady of Lyons." Sat. R. 56 : 571.

in " Pygmalion and Galatea." (F. Wedmore) Acad. 24 : 440.

in " Romeo and Juliet." (Lord Lytton) 19th Cent. 17 : 879 (D.'84). (G. E. Humphreys) National 4 : 819 (F.'85).

in " Winter's Tale." Poet Lore 1 : 92 (F.'89). Sat. R. 64 : 388. (W. Archer) The. n. s. 10 : 214. (H. Luders) Amer. 17 : 216.

" Memories." Dial (Ch.) 20 : 265 (My. 1,'96).

(Anderson, Mary). Girlhood of an Actress. No. Am. 161 : 575 (N.'95).

Extracts from " Memories." L. H. J. (D. '95, Ja. & F. '96).

(Anderson, R. B.) Henrik Ibsen. Amer. 4 : 8.

(Andrews, Maud.) Bernhardt, Terry, and Duse. New Bohemian 2 : 184 (My.'96).

(Angus, J. K.) A Plea for the Writers of Modern Burlesque. Belgra. 79 : 196 (O.'92).

" Antony and Cleopatra." (O. F. Emerson) Poet Lore 2 : 71, 125, 188.

Comradeship of. (S. E. Pearl) Poet Lore 4 : 217 (Ap.'92).

Characters of. (H. S. Wilson) The. n. s. 9 : 59, 127.

Stage History of. The. n. s. 16 : 267.

See also " Cleopatra," etc.

"**As You Like It**," Daly's Co. in. *See "Daly's Co.," etc.*
Jaques and the Duke. (J. Addis) St. James 46: 402.
Plot of. (C. A. Wurtzburg) Poet Lore 3: 341. *See also "Rosalind," etc.*

(**Ashhurst**, R. L.) "King Henry IV." Poet Lore 1: 367.

Ashwell, Lena. The. n. s. 22: 181 (O.'93).

(**Aspden**, Hartley.) Miss Fortesque. The. n. s. 22: 181 (O.'93).

Audience, Duty of an. (E. Faithful) The. '79, 2: 76. (E. Coxon) The. '86, 1: 74.

Audiences. All the Year 38: 273.
An Actor on. The. n. s. 27: 249 (Mr.'96).
American. (H. Irving) Fortn. 43: 197. Same art. Ecl. M. 104: 475; also Liv. Age 164: 705.
American, and Actors. (J. Hatton) The. '81, 1: 257.
Attitudes of. (Lady Pollock) The. '80, 1: 81.
Is Courtesy Extinct Among? (L. Smith) The. n. s. 14: 10.
Modern. (F. C. Broughton) The. '78, 2: 36.
Halls, Theatres, and. (D. Boucicault) No. Am. 149: 429 (O.'89).

(**Austen**, J.) Plays, First Nights of. The. '79, 1: 367.

(**Austin**, Alfred) Divorce between Literature and Stage. National 2: 608 (Ja.'84).
Cossa Pietro, the Dramatist. Fortn. 37: 49.

(**Austin**, L. F.) My First Critique. The. '78, 2: 362.
Henry Irving. Victoria 28: 441.
Theophilus Cibber and Garrick. The. '78, 2: 121.

Australian Drama. (D. Robertson) The. n. s. 9: 23.
Theatres. (J. F. Hogan) The. n. s. 14: 296 (D.'89).
(A. Brereton) The. n. s. 15: 40 (Ja.'90).

"**Author**! Author!" The. n. s. 27: 313 (Je.'96).

Author-Critic. *See "Criticism," etc.*

Author-Manager. *See "Manager," etc.*

(**Ball**, W. T. W.)   Irving's Influence on the American Stage.
  N. Eng. M. n. s. 10 : 173 (Ap.'94).

(**Ballantyne**. E.)   Impressions of Australian Drama. The. n.s.
  19 : 186 (Ap. '92).
  Continental Music Halls. The. n. s. 17 : 121 (Mr. '91).
  The Stall, the Pit, and the Critic. The. n. s. 16 : 20 (Jl. '90).

Ballet. All the Year 12 : 94. (M. E. Hawcis) St. Paul
  12 : 324.
  and Stage Morality. Blackw. 105 : 354. Same art. Ecl.
  M. 72 : 620.
  History of. (J. B. Matthews) Appleton 19 : 306.
  English. Ev. Sat. 14 : 429.

Ballets and Ballet Dancers. (D. Cook) Belgra. 25 : 522.

Ballet-Girls of Paris. Lond. Soc. 17 : 25, 181. Ev. Sat. 9 : 55.

Ballet-Dancers. Chamb. J. 19 : 387.

(**Ballou**, W. H.)   Joseph Jefferson at Home. Cosmop. 7 : 121.

(**Bamflyde**, H.)   Acting as a Fine Art. The. n. s. 12 : 127
  (S. '88).

Bancroft, S. B. The. '83, 1 : 169.

Bancroft, Mrs. S. B. C., *née* Marie Wilton. The. 85, 1 : 49,
  75, 115.
  Mr. and Mrs. Ath., 88, 1 : 493 (Ap. 21). Sat. R. 65 :
  473 (Ap. 21, '88). Westm. 129 : 629. (C. Howard) The.
  n. s. 11 : 250; 12 : 57. (L. C. Cameron) Lond. Soc.
  53 : 601.

(**Bandmann**, D. E.)   German Stage. Macmil. 33 : 430.

(**Barca**, de la, Mme.)   The Standard Drama. No. Am. 39 : 329.

(**Barclay**, Thos.)   Retirement of M. Got. The. n. s. 25 : 20
  (Ja. '95).

(**Barham**, R. N.)   "Merchant of Venice." Bentley 11 : 429.

(**Barlow**, G.)   Talent and Genius on the Stage. Contemp.
  62 : 385 (S. '92).
  Henry Irving and the English Drama. New R. 7 : 665
  (D. '92).

Barnabee, Henry Clay. (F. A. Munsey) Munsey 12: 612
(Mr. '95).

(Barnard, C.) How to Introduce New Plays. Critic 3: 389.
Science on the Stage. Dr. Mirror 23: 575 (J. 4,'90).

Barnett, Henry Hyam Vincent. The. n. s. 20: 24 (Jl. '92).

Baron, Michel. All the Year 39: 160.

(Barr, Amelia E.) Shakspere, Illustrated by Ballads. Harper
63: 52 (D. '80).
Early Home of Adelaide Neilson. Lippinc. 30: 623.
Shakspere as a Temperance Leader. Leisure Hour
35: 29.

(Barrère, Camille.) Dramas of Victor Hugo. Macmil. 30:
281 (Ag. '74).

Barrett, Lawrence. Critic 18: 169. (T. E. Shea) Donahue
(S. '96).
Acting of. Sat. R. 57: 509.
and his Plays. (G. E. Montgomery) Cent. 5: 954
(Ap. '84).

(Barrett, Lawrence.) Vicissitudes of the Drama. No. Am.
146: 203.
Edwin Forrest. Cent. 2: 468.
Success on the Stage. No. Am. 135: 580.

Barrett, Wilson. The. '83, 1: 33. (A. Brereton) The. '82,
2: 161. The. n. s. 27: 129 (Mr. '96).
and his Work. (J. Coleman) Longm. 7: 63.
as Claude Melnotte. The. n. s. 11: 201.
as Friar John. The. '81, 2: 41, 240.
as Hamlet. Lippinc. 45: 580. Sat. R. 58: 527, 595.
(H. Norman) Nation 39: 396.
in "The Acrobat." The. n. s. 17: 259.
in "Golden Ladder." (M. de Meusiaux) The. n. s. 11: 85.
in "Lights of London." The. n. s. 17: 150.
in "Stranger." The. n. s. 17: 142.
in "Pharaoh." The. n. s. 20: 202 (N.'92).
"Sign of the Cross." (E. A. Gowing) Lond. Soc. 69: 472.

3

Beaumont, Francis, and Fletcher. (C. C. Clarke) Gent. M. n.s.
7: 27. (J. Pyne) Nat. Q. 23: 302. (E. P. Whipple) Am.
Whig R. 4: 68, 131. Liv. Age 14: 385. Fraser
22: 189; 41: 321. Ed. M. 12: 174. Temp. Bar
42: 460. Brit. Q. 2: 250. (J. R. Lowell) Harper
85: 757 (O. '92).
and Fletcher and Contemporaries. (W. Spalding) Ed. R.
73: 209.
and Fletcher, "A King and No King." (L. M. Griffiths)
Poet Lore. 3: 169.

(Beck, P.) Realism. The.'83, 1: 127.

(Bede, C.) Reminiscences of Charlotte Cushman. Belgra.
29: 333.

(Bedford, H.) T. Salvini. Month 27: 288.

Behind the Scenes. (F. C. Burnand) Fortn. 43: 84. Same
art. Ecl. M. 104: 409. (A. Fleming) Harper 34: 114
(D.'66). (C. W. Stoddard) Atlan. 34: 527 (N.'84).
(T. C. Haliburton) Bentley 8: 458. (G. A. Sala)
Belgra. 7: 197 Chamb. J. 34: 129. Atlan. 71: 856
(Je. '93). Galaxy, 13: 404. (G. Kobbé) Scrib. 4: 435
(O.'88). Lond. Soc. 4: 385. Chamb. J. 44: 593, 51:
638; 52: 178.
at Drury Lane. All the Year 60: 302.
at the Lyceum. (P. Fitzgerald) Belgra. 44: 335.
Secret Regions of the Stage. (O. Logan.) Harper 48:
628 (O.'88). Tinsley 10: 285.

(Bell, E. I.) Stage as a School of Art. Art. J. 36: 141.

(Bell, R.) Privileges of the Stage. St. James, 1: 317.
First Theatre in London. Once a Week 1: 464 (Same,
Liv. Age 64: 294).

Bellew, Kyrle. The. '82, 2: 257, 263. The. n. s. 20: 125.
(S.'92).

(Bellows, I. F.) Moral Element in Fanny Kemble's "Records of Later Life." Univ. R. 19: 115.

(**Belmont, F.**) Dumas, *fils.* Tinsley 35 : 35.

(**Benjamin, P.**) Plays of James Sheridan Knowles. No. Am. 40 : 141.

(**Benjamin, S. G. W.**) Passion Play of Persia. Harper 72 : 460 (F.'86).

(**Bennett, J. B.**) History of Theatrical Amusements. Ex. Hist. Soc. 2 : 211.

Benson, F. R. as Hamlet. The. n. s. 15 : 212. Sat. R. 69 : 315.

Berringer, Esmé. The. n. s. 27 : 283 (My.'96).

(**Bernard, J.**) Retrospection of American Drama. Manhat. 3 : 604.

Bernhardt, Sarah. The. '79, 2 : 4. Sat. R. 64 : 120. Harper 51 : 635 ; 62 : 306. (W. Archer) National 7 : 770 (Ag.'86). (J. B. Matthews) Amer. 1 : 92. (C. Clark) Chap-Book 5 : 89 (Je. 15, '96). (A. Meynell) Art J. 40 : 134. (M. White, Jr.) Munsey 14 : 323 (D.'95). (M. G. Van Rensselaer) Lippinc. 27 : 180 (F.'81). (R. G. White) Atlan. 47 : 95. The. n. s. 25 : 321 (Je.'95).

Terry and Duse. (M. Andrews) New Bohemian 2 : 184 (My.'96).

and Duse, in " Magda." (G. B. Shaw) Sat. R. 79 : 787 (Je. 15, '95).

as Cleopatra. Critic 18 ; 113. Sat. R. 73 : 654. Art J. 44 : 198 (Jl.'92).

as Joan of Arc. Critic 19 : 269.

as Lady Macbeth. Sat. R. 57 : 777. Same, Critic 5 : 8.

as Ophelia. Critic 61 : 365.

in Boston Book Store. Critic 13 : 241 (My.10,'90).

in " Hernani." (A. G. Segswick) Nation 31 : 383.

in " La Tosca." Critic 18 : 85. (K. Venning) The. n. s. 11 : 46 ; 12 : 97.

in Oporto. (O. Crawfurd). Acad. 21 : 321 (My.'6, 82).

in " Phèdre." (A. G. Segswick) Nation 31 : 399.

in " Ruy Blas." The. '79, 1 : 283.

Rachel and. (J. P. Simpson) The. '80, 2 : 23.

(**Bernhardt,** Sarah.) Art of Make-Up. Cosmopolitan (Mr. '96).

(**Besant,** Walter.) J. B. P. Molière and his Satire. Temp. Bar 33: 83.
　　J. B. P. Molière and his Troupe. Temp. Bar. 32: 374. Same, Liv. Age 110: 163.

(**Bettany,** W. A. L.) Dramatic Criticism and the Renascent Drama. The. n. s. 19: 277 (Je.'92).
　　Winifred Emery. The. n. s. 22: 301 (D '93).
　　Five Years of Progress. The. n. s. 23: 241 (My.'94).
　　Four Character Comedians. The. 22: 9 (Jl.'93).
　　Four Leading Men. The. 20: 109 (S.'92).
　　Modern Drama as viewed by Mr. Jones. The. 22: 203 (O.'93).
　　Policy of Our Leading Managers. The. n. s. 23: 181 (Ap.'94).
　　H. Beerbohm Tree. The. n. s. 19: 69 (F.'92).
　　Mr. and Mrs. Tree at the Haymarket. The. 23: 75 (F.'94).

(**Bibb,** G. C.) Lady Macbeth. Western 1: 287 (My.'75).

(**Bilson,** W. W.) Shylock. The Story of the Bond. Pop. Sci. Mo. 20: 369.

Biographia Dramatica. Blackw. 89: 212.

Biography, Jones's. Quart. 7: 282.

(**Bispham,** W.) Edwin Booth, Memories and Letters. Cent. 47: 132, 240 (N. & D.'93).

Björnson, Björnsterne. (R. Buchanan) Contemp. 21: 45. Appleton 11: 104. Scrib. 20: 336.
　　and Ibsen. (Mrs. A. Tweedie) Temp. Bar 98: 536 (Ag. '93).
　　Dramas of. Macmil. 61; 130. (H. H. Boyesen) No. Am. 116: 109.

(**Björnson**, Björnsterne.) Works of Ibsen. Forum 21 : 318 (My. '96).

(**Black**, Pearl.) Victorien Sardou. Lippinc. 10: 314.

(**Blackburn**, H.) Passion Play at Ober Ammergau. Once a Week 23 : 35.

(**Blackburn**, V.) Eleanora Duse. New R. 13 : 39 (Jl. '95).

(**Blanchard**, L.) The Madness of Hamlet. Colburn 68 : 93.

(**Blind**, K.) Theatres in the Time of Shakspere. Acad. 33 : 390.

(**Bloede**, G.) John McCullough. Western 6: 352, 472. Tennyson's "Harold." Western 3: 430.

(**Blouet**, Paul) ("Max O'Rell"). Modern English Stage through French Spectacles. Dr. Mirror 23: 580 (F. 8, '90).

(**Bluff**, Oliver.) Tree as Hamlet. The. n. s. 19 : 175 (Ap. '92).

(**Bok**, Edw. W.) Mary Anderson as She is To-Day. L. H. J. (Mr. '96).

Bolton, Lavinia Fenton, Duchess of. The. n. s. 20 : 168 (O. '92).

Bond, Jessie. The. n. s. 25 : 67 (F. '95).

(**Bond**, R. W.) Carr's "King Arthur." Fortn. 63 : 703 (My. '95). Stratford Festival. Macmil. 69 : 451 (Ap. '94).

(**Bonjour**, C.) French Dramatic Opinions. Colburn 52 : 363.

Booth, Barton. Colburn 54 : 355. and the Actors of Queen Anne's Days. Temp. Bar 53 : 407.

Booth, Edwin.   Harper 22 : 702 (Ap.'61).   Harper 27 : 855 ;
30 : 673.   Foster Mo. Ref. 3 : 17.   Critic 22 : 384 (Ag.
'93).   Public Opinion 15 : 284 (Je. 17,'93).   (J. Jefferson) Critic 25 : 210 (S. 29,'94).   (H. A. Clapp)
Atlan. 72 : 307 (S.'93).   (J. R. Lows) Nation 56 : 434
(Je. 15.'93).   (E. C. Stedman) Atlan. 17 : 585.   (W.
Winter) Harper 63 : 61 (Je.'81).   (L. Hutton) Harper's W. (Je. 17,'93.)   (L. C. Calhoun) Galaxy (with
portrait) 7 : 77.   (H. C. Pedder) Manhat. 3 : 295.   Colburn (with portrait) 168 : 64.

Across America with.   (Elizabeth Robins) Univ. R.
7 : 375 (Jl.'90).

An Actor's Recollections of.   (Barton Hill) Dr. Mirror
37 : 939 (Xmas,'96).

Acting of.   (O. B. Frothingham) Nation 2 : 395.

and J. B.   Sat. R. 53 : 273.   (A. B. Clarke) Cent. 2 :
468.

the Friendship of, and Julia Ward Howe.   (F. M. H. Hall)
N. Eng. M. n. s. 9 : 315 (N.'93).

as Bertuccio.   Sat. R. 54 : 148 (Jl. 29,'82).

as Hamlet.   Appleton 14 : 657, 689.   Ev. Sat. (with portrait) 9 : 258, 273.   The. 2 : 351, '80.

as King Lear.   The. n. s. 20 : 284 (D.'92).

as Richelieu.   The. 2 : 75, '82.   Harper 42 : 296 (Ja.'71).
Ev. Sat. (with portrait) 9 : 402, 409 ; 10 : 80, 91.

Mrs. Grossmann's Recollections of.   (E. A. Barron) Dial
(Ch.) 18 : 17 (Ja. 1,'95).

in Chicago.   Lakeside 9 : 349.

in England.   Harper 63 : 466 (Ag.'81).

in Germany.   (T. Baker) Nation 36 : 358.

Letters of.   (Edwina Booth Grossmann) Century 48 : 803
(O.'94).

"The Players'" Tribute to.   Critic 23 ; 327 (N. 18,'93).

Memories and Letters of.   (Wm. Bispham) Cent. 47 :
132, 240 (N. & D.'93).

Memories of.   (Mrs. D. P. Bowers) Cal. Ill. 5 : 471 (Mr.
'94).

Booth, Edwin, Memory of, An Actor's. (John Malone) Forum 15: 594 (Jl.'93).

On and Off the Stage. (Adam Badeau) McClure 1: 255 (Ag. '93).

Poem on. (Ina Coolbrith) Cal. Ill. 4: 364 (Ag.'93).

Portrait of, Sargent's at "The Players'" (Poem). (T. B. Aldrich) Harper 82: 489 (F.'91).

Booth, Junius Brutus. (I. C. Pray) Galaxy 2: 158. All the Year 36: 77.

and Edwin. Sat. R. 53: 273. (A. B. Clarke) Cent. 2: 468.

(Botkin, A. C.) Maiming of Hamlet. Lakeside 9: 444.

Boucicault, Dion. Acad. 38: 278. Critic 17: 158. Sat. R. 70: 373. (S. Fiske) The. n. s. 24: 301 (D.'94). (A. C. Wheeler) Arena 3: 47 (D.'90).

"Formosa." The. n. s. 18: 27.

"London Assurance." The. n. s. 17: 41.

"Shaughraun." Harper 51: 293 (Jl.'75).

(Boucicault, Dion.) Education of an Actor. No. Am. 147: 435.

Future of American Drama. Arena 2: 641.

Art of Dramatic Composition. No. Am. 126: 430.

Coquelin and Irving. No. Am. 145: 158.

Decline of the Drama. No. Am. 125: 235.

Début and Early Days as a Dramatist. No. Am. 148: 454, 584.

Leaves from a Dramatist's Diary. No. Am. 149: 228 (Ag.'89).

Theatres, Halls, and Audiences. No. Am. 149: 429 (O. '89).

A New Cipher. Dr. Mirror 23: 593 (M. 10,'90).

The New Departure. Dr. Mirror 22: 569 (N. 23,'89).

Bouffé, Marie. Sat. R. 66: 603 (N. 24,'88). All the Year 68: 372.

Bourchier, Arthur. The. n. s. 25: 95 (F.'95).

(**Bowen, F.**)   Emendation of Shakspere.   No. Am. 78 : 371.

(**Bowen, G. S.**)   Realism in Plays.   Colo. 169 : 10.

(**Bowers**, Mrs. D. P.)   Memories of Edwin Booth.   Cal. Ill.
5 : 471 (Mr.'94).

(**Boyes**, J. F.)   Dutton Cook.   Longm. 3 : 179 (D.'83).

Boyesen, H. H.   On Ibsen.   Spec. 72 : 652 (My. 12,'94).   Sat.
R. 78 : 359 (S. 29, '94).

(**Boyesen**, H. H.)   Ibsen.   "Comedy of Love."   Dial (Ch.) 14 :
132 (Mr. 1,'93).
"Doll's House."   Cosmopolitan 16 : 84 (N.'93).
"Peer Gynt."   Chaut. 17 : 293 (Je.'93).
"Wild Duck."   Dial (Ch.) 15 : 137 (S. 16.'93).
"Little Eyolf."   Chap-Book 2 : 247 (F.'95).
Henrik Ibsen.   Cent. 16 : 794 (Mr.'90).
Drama of Revolt.   Bookman 1 : 384.
Dramas of Björnson.   No. Am. 116 : 109.

Braddon, Miss M. E.   (H. James, Jr.) Nation 1 : 593.   Same
art. Liv. Age 77 : 99.   (Brenan, J. C.) Sharpe 39 : 86.

(**Braddon**, Miss.)   Hermann Sudermann.   National 21 : 751
(Ag.'93).
Sudermann's "Die Ehre."   The. n. s. 25 : 131 (Mr.'95).

(**Brain**, Ernest.)   French View of the English Stage.   The.
n. s. 26 : 195 (O.'95).
Modern German Drama.   The. n. s. 25 : 84 (F.'95).
Salvini's Reminiscences.   The. n. s. 26 : 16 (Jl.'95).
A French View of Shakspere.   The. n. s. 27 : 208 (Ap.
'96).

Brandon, Olga.   The. n. s. 29 : 4 (Jl.'96).

Brazil.   Theatre at Para.   Harper 57 : 357 (Ag.'78).

(**Brereton**, Austin.)   Wilson Barrett.   The.'82, 2 : 161.
Mrs. Eliz. Barry.   The.'86, 2 : 264.
Drama in New York.   The.'84, 1 : 24.
John Henderson.   The.'86, 1 : 303.

(**Bryce,** Jas.) Sardou's "Cleopatra." Contemp. 47: 266
(F. '85). Same art. Liv. Age. 164: 733 (Mr. '85).

Buchanan, Robt. (G. H. Lewes) Fortn. 1: 443. (G. B.
Smith) Contemp. 22: 873.
(A. M. Symington) Good Words 19: 15. Tinsley 19: 89.
"The Charlatan." Sat. R. 77: 94 (Ja. 27, '94).

(**Buchanan,** Robt.) Modern Drama and Its Critics. Contemp.
56: 908.
H. Caine and.) What is a Tragedy? Acad. 34: 15-30.
How to Produce a Play at Small Outlay. The. n. s.
29: 9 (Jl. '96).
B. Björnson. Contemp. 21: 45.
Ethics of Play Licensing. The. n. s. 27: 254 (Mr. '96).

(**Buckley,** J. M.) Moral Influence of the Stage. No. Am.
136: 581.

Buffoons, Stage. (E. Robins) Atlan. 51: 529.
Clowns, Pantomime. (G. Turner) The. '84, 1: 194.
Fools of Shakspere. (T. R. Slicer) N. Eng. M. n. s.
12: 374 (My. '95).
Harlequins, Concerning. '81, 1: 10.
in Extremis. (D. J. Anderson) The. '79, 1: 103.
Harlequins, History of. Temp. Bar 43: 202.
Harlequinade. Chamb. J. 26: 340.

Bulwer, E. L. *See "Lord Lytton."*
The Drama of Revolt. Bookman 1: 384 (Jl. '95).

(**Bunce,** O. B.) Some of Our Actors. Galaxy 5: 165.

Burbage, Rich'd. Temple Bar. 53: 252.

Burlesque, Age of. (R. G. White) Galaxy 8: 256. (Brenan,
J. C.) Sharpe 39: 86. (W. D. Howells) Atlan. 23: 635.
American Burlesque. (L. Hutton) Harper 81: 59 (Je.
'90.)
The Founders of. Temple Bar 29: 318.
Modern, A Plea for the Writers of. (J. K. Angus)
Belgra. 79: 196 (O. '92).

Burlesque, The New and the Old.   St. Paul's 4: 698.
 The, and the Beautiful.   (R. H. Horne) Contemp. 18: 390.
 Writers of, in England.   (C. C. Clarke) Gent. M. n. s.
   4: 167.
 An Old.   (D. Cook) The. '82, 2: 267.
 The Old and the New.   (W. D. Adams) The. n. s. 27: 144
   (Mr. '96).
 Uses and Abuses of.   (T. Heyward) Tinsley 37: 477.

Burlesques.   Cornh. 4: 167.

Burletta, What is a?   (D. Cook) Once a Week 12: 233.

Burnand, Frank Cowley.   With portrait.   The. '79, 1: 34;
   '83, 1: 105.

(Burnand, F. C.)   A School for Dramatic Art.   (Reply to H.
   Aïdé) 19th Cent. 11: 753 (My.'82).
 Behind the Scenes.   Fortn. 43: 84.   Same art. Ecl. M.
   104: 409.
 Councils and Comedians.   Fortn. 44: 370.
 Reminiscences of the Royalty.   The. n. s. 27: 70 (F.
   '96).
 Ghost in Hamlet.   Month 64: 64.

Burroughs, Marie.   (Robt. Edgarton) Lippinc. 51: 363
   (Mr. '93).

(Burton, R.)   Maurice Maeterlinck.   Atlan. 74: 672 (N. '94).

Burton's Theatre, N. Y., Fracas at.   The.'82, 2: 15.

(Bushby, Mrs.)   Passion Play at Ober Ammergau.   Colburn
   147: 288.

Butler, Mrs.   *See " Fanny (or Frances) Kemble."*

(Byron, H. J.)   Growls from the Playwright.   The. '80, 1: 20.
 Going on the Stage.   The. '79, 2: 130.
 Causes of Failures of.   The. '79, 1: 221.

Byron and Shelley on the Character of Hamlet.   Colburn
   29: 327.

Caine, Lilly Hall.   The. n. s. 23 : 250 (My. '94).

(Caine, Thomas Henry Hall.)   Mrs. Oliphant's Life of R. B.
    Sheridan. Acad. 24 : 271.
    Art of Shakspere. Contemp. 43 : 883. Same art. Ecl. M.
    101 : 240.
    Coleridge's Lectures on Shakspere.   Acad. 25 : 19.
    Supernatural in Shakspere.   Colburn 165 : 1029.
    What is a Tragedy?   Acad. 34 : 15.

(Calcraft, John William.)   *See " Cole."*

(Calhoun, L. C.)   Edwin Booth.   Galaxy 7 : 77.

Calls, Stage.   (G. Turner) The. '84, 1 : 296.

(Calvert, W.)   Annals of the Bath Stage.   The. 24 : 292;
    25 : 13, 175.
    Chas. Wyndham as David Garrick.   The. n. s. 18 : 9.

(Cameron, H. L.)   The Bancrofts.   Lond. Soc. 53 : 601.

" Camille."   *See "Dumas, fils."*

(Campbell, L.)   Notes on " King Lear."   National 12 : 492.

(Campbell, Mrs. Patrick.)   The. n. s. 25 : 292 (My.'95).
    The. n. s. 22 : 92 (Ag.'93).

Canada,   Private Theatricals in.   Harper 63 : 221 (Jl.'81).

(Capes, F. M.)   Popular Representation of Shakspere.   Month
    57 : 69.

(Cargill, Alex.)   Shakspere as an Actor.   Scribner 9 : 613
    (My.'91).

(Carlyle, T.)   German Playwrights.   For. R. 3 : 94.

(Carpenter, Fred'k Ives.)   An American Endowed Theatre.
    Dial (Ch.) 21 : 182 (O. 1, '96).

(Carpenter, Geo. Rice.)   Henrik Ibsen.   Scribner 5 : 404
    (Ap.'89).

(Carpenter, W. H.)   Freytag on the Technique of the Drama.
    Bookman 1 : 315 (Je.'95).
    Bibliography of H. Ibsen.   Bookman 1 : 275.

Carr, J. Comyns. "King Arthur." Sat. R. 79: 93 (Ja. 19, '95). (R. W. Bond) Fortn. 63: 703 (My. '95).
English Actors of Yesterday and To-day. Fortn. 39: 221.

(Carroll, A. L.) A Very Old Play. Galaxy 2: 530.

(Carson, Murray.) The. n. s. 23: 266 (My.'94).
Collaboration. The. n. s. 28: 85 (Ag.'96).

(Carson, R. Claude.) A Plea for the Innocuous. The. n. s. 25: 154 (Mr.'95).

(Castelé, W. R.) Shakspere's Cordelia. Ecl. M. 14: 517.

Cavendish, Ada. The. '82, 1: 39, 125; 85, 1: 159, 204. (F. Wedmore) Acad. 48: 302 (O. 12,'95).

(Cayvan, Georgia.) Theatre Days in Japan. Dr. Mirror, 37: 939 (Xmas '96).

Cecil, Arthur. The. n. s. 26: 33 (Jl.'95).

Celebrities, Bygone. (R. H. Horne) Gent. M. n. s. 6: 247, 660; 7: 88, 468.

Censorship of the Drama. Sat. R. 79: 280 (Mr. 2, '95).
Colburn 70: 345. All the Year 76: 294 (Mr.'95).
(W. Archer) New R. 6: 566 (My.'92). (A. Goodrich) The. n. s. 19: 232 (My.'92). (G. Moore) New R. 3: 354. The. '78, 2: 259, 332. Westm. 121: 328.
(R. Buchanan) The. n. s. 27: 254 (Mr. '96). All the Year 33: 79. All the Year 32: 344, 391. Chamb. J. 26: 313. Same art. Liv. Age 52: 26. Chamb. J. 39: 158; 50: 263. Dub. Univ. 68: 525, 69: 243.
The Censorship of Plays. The. n. s. 25: 193. (Apr. '95).
Cheap Theatres and the Lord Chamberlain. (A. B. Reach) Peop. J. 3: 97.
Touching the Lord Chamberlain. (Chas. Dickens 2nd) The. n. s. 25: 10 (Ja. '95).

(Chapman, John Jay.) Romeo. Atlan. 78: 707 (N.'96).

(**Charlesworth**, H. W.) Playhouse Sonnets. Canad. M.
    1 : 558 (S. '93).
    Some Modernisms on the Stage. Canad. M. 1 : 43 (Mr.
    '93).

"**Charley's Aunt**" on the Continent. (E. J. Goodman;
    H. H. Fyfe) The. n. s. 25 : 338 (Je. '95).

(**Chevalier**, Albert.) Costers and Music Halls. Eng. Illust.
    10 : 479 (Ap.'93).

(**Chiarini**, G.) Two Legends of "Merchant of Venice."
    Chaut. 17 702 (S. '93).

(**Child**, Theo.) Comédie Française. Harper 74 : 691 (Ap.'87).
    Drama of the 16th Century. Amer. 5 : 334.
    French Translations of " Hamlet." The. '81, 2 : 271.
    " Hamlet " in Paris. Poet Lore 2 : 557 (N. '90).
    " Othello " in Paris. Poet Lore 1 : 301, 362 (Jl. & Ag.
    '89).
    Playwrights of Paris. Contemp. 51 : 712.
    Washington on the French Stage. Lippinc. 29 : 293
    (Mr.'82).

Child Life in Shakspere. (M. L. Griffin) Irish Mo.
    19 : 434.

Children, Theatre. Sunday M. 19 : 121.

Children on the Stage. (A. Hornblow) Munsey 12 : 32
    (O. '94).

Chinese Drama. Quart. 16 : 396. All the Year 13 : 29.
    (G. Adams) 19th Cent. 37 : 497 (Mr.'95). (B.
    K. Douglas) Contemp. 37 : 123. Same art. Ecl. M.
    94 : 349.

Chinese Theatre. Spec. 59 : 1683. Cornh. 9 ; 297. (H. B.
    McDonald) Cent. 7 : 27.
    An Afternoon at. Lond. Soc. 31 : 501.
    at San Francisco. Harper 66 : 830 (My.'83).
    In a. (G. H. Fitch) Cent. 2 : 189 (Je.'82). (G. W.
    Lamphigh) Macmil. 57 : 36.

Chinese and Japanese Theatres. (L. Wingate) Murray 2: 89, 232.

(Chorley, J. R.) Notes on Shakspere. Fraser 59: 543. 60: 49, 423.

(Chubb, E. W.) Cicero in the Works of Shakspere. Acad. (Syr.) 5: 108.

Church and Drama. Harper 26: 564 (Mr.'63). (J. Dyer) Penn Mo. 10: 374.
Theatre Denounced by Jeremy Collier. Harper 50: 441 (F.'75).
Stage from a Clergyman's Point of View. (Rev. T. P. Hughes) Forum 20: 695 (F.'96).
Duty of Church as to the Theatre. (N. Hall; H. C. Shuttleworth). Ch. Lit. 11: 302 (S.'94).

Church, and the Stage. Victoria 28: 389.
Stage and the. Godey 131: 127 (Ag.'95).
Theatre and the. (R. Collyer) Critic 3: 277.
Congress on the Drama. The. '78, 2: 255.

Cibber, Colley. "Apology." Spec. 63: 277.
Death and Burial of. (D. Cook) The. '83, 2: 217.
Early Life of. (Lady Lamb) The. '79, 1: 92.

Cicero in the Works of Shakspere. (E. W. Chubb) Acad. (Syr) 5: 108.

(Clapp, H. A.) Edwin Booth. Atlan. 72: 307 (S.'93).
Henry Irving. Atlan. 53: 413.
Wm. Warren. Atlan. 26; 786.
Time in Shakspere's Plays. Atlan. 55: 386, 543.

Claque in Paris Theatres. (L. Kalisch) Ev. Sat. 5: 102.

Claque, La. *See "Applause,"* etc.

(Claretie, J.) French View of Henry Irving. The. '79, 2: 16.

Clarion, Hippolyte. (F. Hawkins) The. '86, 1: 291; 2: 20.

(Claris, L. J.) Henry Irving as Actor and Artist. The. '82, 1: 155.

Clark, Charlotte. (L. Wingate) The. '82, 2 : 40, 85, 137.

(Clarke, C. C.) Philosophers and Jesters of Shakspere.
Gent. M. n. s. 110.
Burlesque Writers of England. Gent. M. n. s. 7 : 557.

(Clarke, H. S.) Stage and Society. The. '85, 2 : 135.
Wm. Moy Thomas. The. '85, 2 : 12.

Clarke, John S. (Wm. Stuart) Lippinc. 28 : 497 (N. '81).
In " The Rivals." The. '85, 2 : 149–167.

(Clarke, M. C.) Simpletons of Shakspere. Sharpe 7 : 217.
Soldiers of Shakspere. Sharpe 9 : 24, 143; 10 : 196,
349.
Individuality of Characters of Shakspere. See " *Shakspere.*"
Admission Prices to Theatres. All the Year 32 : 296.
Lawrence and Kemble's Hamlet. Sharpe 6 : 181.

Clarke, M. G. (A. Croxton) The. n. s. 22 : 121 (S. '93).

(Clarke, S. W.) Sudden Deaths of Actors. The. 19 : 75.

(Clarke, T. W.) Edmund Kean. Knick. 3 : 101.

Claudian on the Stage. (F. Wedmore) Acad. 24 : 404.

(Clayden, P. W.) Macbeth and Lady Macbeth. Fortn. 8 :
153.

Cleopatra, Shakspere's. Tinsley 14 : 22. Fraser 40 : 277.
Cornh. 24 : 344. Same art. Ecl. M. 77 : 582.

Clergy and the Drama. (A. T. Davidson) Macmil. 37 : 497.
See also " Church and the Drama."

(Clifford, Dr.) Can We Have an Ideal Theatre ? Young
Man's (Mr. '93).

Clive, Kitty. (J. F. Molloy) Eng. Illust. 3 : 17.

(Clodd, E.) Miracle Plays. Longm. 15 : 612. Same art.
Ecl. M. 14 : 74. Liv. Age 185 : 431.

Clowns, Harlequins, etc. *See "Buffoons."*

Cobbett, Wm., Comedies of. (G. A. Sala) Belgra. 25 : 465.

Coffin, Hayden. The. n. s. 23: 326 (Je.'94).

(Coghlan, Rose.) Personal Requisites of the Stage. Godey
127: 754 (D.'93).

(Cohn, A.) A. Dumas, *fils*. Bookman (Ja. '96).

(Cole, John William, *pseudonym:* " John William Calcraft.")
French Dramatists and Actors. Dub. Univ. 43: 594,
652.
Writers against the Stage. Dub. Univ. 38: 272.
Dramatic Writers of Ireland. Dub. Univ. 45: 39, 527;
46: 38, 548; 47: 159, 359.
Theatre Royal, Dublin. Dub. Univ. 72: 458, 558.
Leaves from Portfolio of a Manager. *See "Manager."*
Garrick Club Portraits. Dub. Univ. 42: 643; 43:
223, 393.
Improvement in Text of Shakspere. Dub. Univ.
41: 356.

(Coleman, John.) Social Status of the Actor. National 5: 20
(Mr. '85).
Wilson Barrett and his Work. Longm. 7: 63.
Chas. Dillon. Gent. M. n. s. 37: 168.
Reminiscences of Henry Howe. The. n. s. 27: 263
(My. '96).
Personal Reminiscences of Chas. Reade. Lippinc.
34: 146, 234, 354 (Ag., S. and O. '84).
Fact and Fancies about " Macbeth." Gent. M. n. s. 42:
218.
Six Phases in the Life of Molière. The. n. s. 22: 128,
184, 315 (S., O. and D. '93.)
Romance of Drury Lane. Gent. M. n. s. 57: 365 (O. '96).

(Coleridge, Christabel R.) " Faust " from the Room of the
Unlearned. Lond. Soc. 54: 191 (Aug. '88).

Coleridge's Lectures on Shakspere. (T. H. H. Caine) Acad.
25: 19.

(Colin, C.) Björnsterne Björnson. R. of Rs. 6: 411 (N.'92).
5

Collaboration. Sat. R. 56: 564.
(M. Carson.) The. n. s. 28: 85 (Ag. '96).

College Theatricals. (J. K. Hosmer) Nation 10: 6. Blackw.
54: 737. Same art. Ecl. M. 1: 253. Liv. Age 59: 278.
Æschylus. "Agamemnon," acting of, at Oxford in 1880.
(B. L. Gildersleeve) Nation 30: 472.
"Antigone" (Sophocles') at Toronto University. Spec.
72: 369 (Mr. 17, '94).
Aristophanes. "The Frogs," at Oxford. (H. F. Wil-
son) Acad. 41: 237 (Mr. 5, '92). Ath. '92, 1: 318
(Mr. 5, '92). Sat. R. 73: 244. Temp. Bar 95: 238
(Jl. '92). The. 28: 216 (Ap. '92).
As we have them. (E. J. Stevenson) No. Am. 158: 510
(Ap. '94).
Browning's "Stafford" at Oxford Univ. Dram. Soc. Poet
Lore 2: 200 (Ap. '90).
Costumes in the Greek Play at Harvard. (F. D.
Millet) Cent. 1: 65 (N. '81).
Drama in Colleges. (J. K. Hosmer) Atlan. 30: 19
(Jl. '72).
Greek Play at Bradfield College, 1892. (L. Dyer) Nation
55: 26 (Jl. 14, '92).
Greek Play at Cambridge. All the Year 57: 421. (G.
W. Prothero) Cent. 6: 411 (Jl. '84).
Greek Play at Iowa College. "Electra" of Sophocles. R.
of Rs. 2: 174 (S. '92).
Greek Play at Oxford. The. '80, 72: 36.
Greek Play at Oxford, 1892. Sat. R. 73: 244. Ath. '92,
1: 318 (Mr. 5, '92). Temp. Bar 95: 238 (Je. '92).
Greek Play at St. Andrews College. The. '82, 1: 177.
"He Playing She." Scrib. 17: 189.
Latin Play at Harvard. (M. H. Morgan) Harv. Grad.
Mo. 2: 335 (Mr. '94) (Je. '94). (H. W. Haynes) Harv.
Grad. Mo. 2: 515. (J. B. Greenough) New Eng. M. n.s.
10: 491 (Jl. '94). (F. G. Ireland) Educa. R. 8: 54
(Je. '94).

College Theatricals. Ben Jonson. "Epicoene," revival of, at
Harvard College. (G. P. Baker) Harv. Grad. Mo.
3: 493 (Je.'95).
University Theatricals. Dub. Univ. 95: 87.
University Theatre. (G. Riddle) Am. M. 7: 459.

Collier, Jeremy. Theatre denounced by. Harper 50: 441.

(Collier, Robt. Laird.) Henry Irving. Lippinc. 32: 441 (N.'83).

(Collins, M. and J. Lillie.) Madame Modjeska. Temp. Bar
66: 22, 551; 67: 73.

(Collyer, R.) Theatre and the Church. Critic 3: 277.

Colman, Geo., the Elder and the Younger. (H. B. Baker)
Belgra. 46: 187. Same art. Ecl. M. 98: 214.
and D. Garrick, "Clandestine Marriage." (P. H. Fitzgerald) The. 18: 340.

Columbine Question, The. All the Year 35: 390 (J. 22,'76).

Comedians, Among the. (L. C. Davis) Atlan. 19: 750.
of the Age. (W. Davenport Adams) The. n. s. 22: 144
(S. '93).
Attitude of the Church on. Fortn. 44: 370. Same art.
Ecl. M. 105.
Four Characters. (W. A. L. Bettany) The. n. s. 22: 9
(Jl.'93).

Comédie Française. (T. Child) Harper 74: 691 (Ap. '87).
(Ed. Rose) The.'79, 1: 311. (C. Hervey) The.'84, 2: 1.
A Company of Actors. (J. B. Matthews) Scrib. 16: 837
(O. '78).
(A. Strobel) Murray. 6: 334. Same art. Ecl. M.
113: 335.
and the English Stage. Dub. Univ. 94: 340.
Foyer of. (F. Hawkins) The. '79, 1: 360.
of To-day. (A. D. Vandam) New R. 9: 314 (S. '93).
Origin of. (F. Hawkins) The. '79, 1: 286.
Visit to. The. '79, 1: 277.
Women of. (E. A. De Wolfe) Cosmop. 11: 643.

Comedies, Old. Harper 73: 308 (Jl. '86); 75: 309 (Jl.'88).

Comedy.　Monitor 2 : 45.

　　A Half Forgotten.　(Laurence Hutton.)　Dr. Mirror 23 : 584 (M. 8,'90).

　　Comic Dramatists of the Restoration.　(J. Pyne) National Q. 34 : 306.

　　Decline of.　Sat. R. 68 : 457.

　　Modern.　(J. B. Matthews) Princ. n. s. 11 : 273. Blackw. 19 : 46.

　　Modern Tendencies of.　(Chas. Wyndham) No. Am. 149 : 607 (D. '89).

　　The Prize.　(D. Cook) The. '82, 2 : 65.

　　Two Thousand Years of.　(C. S. A. Herford) N. Eng. M. 53 : 441.

　　Woman in.　(C. T. Congdon) Harper 37 : 507 (S. '68).

"Comedy of Errors."　All the Year 48 : 390.　(A. Lang) Harper 82 : 550.　(D. J. Snider) Western 2 : 296.　Once a Week 14 : 380.

　　The "Comedy of Errors" at Gray's Inn.　(Arthur à Becket) The. n. s. 27 : 31 (Ja. '96).

Comic Opera, French.　Temp. Bar 47 : 493.

　　The Decline of.　(W. D. Adams) The. n. s. 26 : 202 (O. '95).

Composition, Situation and Character.　Ev. Sat. 13 : 229. Cornh. 26 : 155.

　　Decline of.　Blackw. 9 : 279.

　　Dramas for Music, How to Write.　(F. A. Laidlaw) The. n. s. 18 : 67.

　　Dramatic, Art of.　(D. Boucicault) No. Am. 126 : 40. Oxford Prize Essay 1 : 167.

　　Dramatic Construction (S. Grundy) The. '81, 1 : 208.

　　Methods of English Playwrights.　Nation 38 : 543.

　　Novels, Dramatization of.　(J. B. Matthews) Longm. 14 : 588 (O. '89).

　　Playwriting.　(A. Hennequin) Forum 8 : 705 (F. '90). (J. Littlejohn) Irish Mo. 17 : 356.　(C. E. Meetkerke) The. 25 : 156.　(S. Rosenfeld) Author 3 : 142.　Gent. M. n. s. 49 : 423 (O. '92).

(Cook, Edw. Dutton.) Players and Parsons. The. '78, 2: 269.

    Rachel. Gent. M. n. s. 25 : 188.

    Reader of Plays. Belgra. 36 : 432.

    Shakspere Festival, 1864. Once a Week 10 : 104.

    Stage Properties. Belgra. 35 : 282.

    Stage Thunder. Once a Week 14 : 685.

    Strange Actors. Belgra. 45 : 51. Same art. Appleton 26 : 267.

    Strange Players. Ecl. M. 97 : 337.

    Thackeray and the Theatre. Longm. 4 : 409. Same art. Critic 5 : 80, 92.

    The Prize Comedy. The. '82, 2 : 65.

    The Right to Hiss. The. '83, 2 : 178.

    "Twelfth Night." Once a Week 14 : 65.

    W. A. Conway and Mrs. Piozzi. Gent. M. n. s. 27 : 538 (N. '81).

(Cook, K.) Ancient Drama and Modern Novel. Dark Blue 3 : 709.

Cooke. Kean's Monument to. Harper 44 : 188 (Ja. '72).

Cooke, Geo. Fred'k. Harper 35 : 23 (Jl. '67); 63 : 874 (N. '76). The. '82, 2 : 279. Mus. 43 : 508. Portf. (Den.) 9 : 532. Temp. Bar 50 : 189. Same art. Ecl. M. 89 : 197. (W. Dunlap) Anal. M. 1 : 404, 466.

(Cooke, J.) Astrology of Shakspere. Macmil. 51 : 462. Same art. Liv. Age. 165 : 281.

Cooper, Thos. A. Chamb. J. 49 : 473. Ecl. M. 62 : 214. Lond. M. 38 : 445. Howitt 3 : 226, 242.

Coppée, François. (T. Beaugeard) The. n. s. 27 : 277 (My. '96).

Cordelia. (W. R. Castelé) Ecl. M. 14 : 517.

"Coriolanus." (D. J. Snider) Western 1 : 695, 771. (J. M. Street) N. Eng. M. 51 : 260.

    on the Stage. (A. Hallam) The. '79, 2 : 22.

Craig, Ailsa. The. n. s. 26 : 219 (O. '95).

(Craik, Mrs. D. M.) Dramatic Art of Present Day. 19th Cent. 416 (S. '86).

(Crane, W. H.) Play-writing from the Actor's Point of View. No. Amer. 157 : 325 (S. '93).

(Crane, W. W.) Allegory in " Hamlet." Poet Lore 3 : 565.

(Crawfurd, Oswald.) Bernhardt in Oporto. Acad. 21 : 321 (My. 6, '82).

(Creighton, C.) Falstaff's Deathbed. Blackw. 145 : 324.

Critic. The Author-Critic. Sat. R. 61 : 503.
>a, and the Critics Criticized. (C. Scott) The. n. s. 13 : 297.
>Dickens as a Dramatic. (D. Cook) Longm. 2 : 29.
>G. H. Lewes as a Dramatic. (W. D. Adams) The. n. s. 27 : 337 (Je. '96).
>Dramatist : Old and New. The. n. s. 26 : 187 (O. '95).

Critics, Dramatic, and the Dramatists. Harper 81 : 152 (Je. '90).
>Dramatic, Duties of. (W. Archer) 19th Cent., 17 : 249 (F. '85).
>Modern Drama and its. (R. Buchanan) Contemp. 56 : 908.
>The Stall, the Pit, and the. (E. Ballantyne) The. n. s. 16 : 20.
>as Actors. (H. Louther) Tinsley 28 : 60.

Criticism, Dramatic. The. 27 : 153. (J. H. McCarthy) Gent. M. n. s. 52 : 313 (Mr. '94). (B. Stoker) No. Am. 158 : 325 (Mr. '94). (W. L. Courtney) Contemp. 64 : 691 (N. '93). Same art. Ecl. M. 132 : 63 (Jl. '94). Amer. 1 : 121. All the Year 71 : 509 (N. 26, '92).
>An Actor's Pet Affectation. (Not to read newspaper criticisms.) The. n. s. 27 : 125 (Mr. '96).
>Dramatic, American. Amer. 1 : 121.
>Dramatic, and the Renascent Drama. (W. A. L. Bettany) The. n. s. 19 : 277 (Je. '92).
>Influence of. (S. J. A. Fitz-Gerald) The. n. s. 24 : 238 (N. '94).

Cushman, Charlotte. The. '78, 2 : 172. Victoria 32 : 468.
All the Year 41 : 102. (G. F. Ferris) Appleton 11 : 353.
(J. D. Stockton) Scrib. 12; 262 (Je.'76). (R. G.
White) Nation : 314. (M. Howitt) Peop. J. 2 : 30-47.
and Macbeth. (G. F. Ferris) Lakeside 7 : 407.
and Rachel. (Mme. de Marguerites) Sharpe 15 : 13.
Remembrances of. (C. Bede) Belgra. 29 : 333.

(Cutter, C. A.) Playwright's Art. Nation 38 : 382.

"Cymbeline." All the Year 53 : 532. Acad. 40 : 460. (D. J.
Snider) J. Spec. Philos. 9 : 172.
at the Lyceum. (R. W. Bond) Fortn. (N. '96).
In a Hindu Playhouse. (H. Littledale) Macmil. 42 : 65.
Same art. Liv. Age 145 : 695.
Lesson of. (H. P. Goddard) Poet Lore 1 : 64.

Daly, Augustin, His Company in " As You Like It." (C.
Howard) The. n. s. 16 : 90.
His Company in "Taming the Shrew." (F. A. Marshall ;
P. Fitzgerald) The. n. s. 12 : 10.
His Company in " Railroad of Love." (P. H. Fitzgerald)
The. n. s. 11 : 315.
Plays in London. Sat. R. 69 : 731 ; 70 : 73, 105.

(Daly, A.) American Drama. No. Am. 142 : 485.

Daly's Stock Co. (L. C. Davis) Lippinc. 32 : 396.

Dancers, English Stage. (W. D. Adams) The. n. s. 25 :
76 (Feb.'95).

Dangers, Fire, Panic, Riot, etc. Brooklyn Theatre Fire. Harper 64 : 466 (F.'82).
Theatres in Peril from Fire. Harper 64 : 788 (Ap.'82).
Theatre Panic. Harper 37 : 708 (O.'68) ; 60 : 788 (Ap.
'80).

(Daniels, J. A.) Some Eccentric Stage Costumes. The. n. s.
20 : 251 (D.'92).

Danish Drama. Fortn. 28 : 1. (W. Archer) Fortn. 53 : 682.

Danish National Theatre. Cornh. 30 : 297.

(Dannreuther, E.) Musical Drama. Macmil. 33 : 80.

(D'Arcy, W.) Her Majesty's Theatre. Belgra. 4 : 416.

Dashwood, Chas. The. n. s. 22 : 247 (D.'93).

(Daudet, Alphonse.) My "First Night." The. n. s. 25 : 299 (Je.'94).

> Toilers of the Stage. The. n. s. 24 : 1 (Jl.'94).

> Drunkenness on the Stage. The. n. s. 24 : 48 (Ag.'94).

(Dauncey, S.) The Stage and Mr. Burnand. Tinsley 36 : 323.

Dauvray, Helen, in "A Scrap of Paper." The. n. s. 19 : 203 (Ap.'92).

Davenport, E. L., Recollections of. (H. P. Goddard) Lippinc. 21 : 463.

(Davenport, Fanny.) Some Childish Memories. Lippinc. 42 : 565 (O.'88).

(Davey, Rich'd.) Beginnings of the Drama in America. National 19 : 802 (Ag.'92).

> Alex. Dumas, *fils.* The. n. s. 27 : 12 (Ja.'96).

> Death of Rachel. The. '80, 1 : 273.

> Italian Drama. No. Am. 19 : 90.

> Italian Stage. Lippinc. 15 : 90.

> M. Arsène Houssaye. The. n. s. 27 : 271 (My.'96).

> Modern Criticism. The. n. s. 26 : 137 (S.'95).

> New "Robert Macaire." The. n. s. 26 : 30 (Jl.'95).

> The Italian Stage. The. '80, 2 : 300.

(Davidson, A. C.) "Ophelia." The. '81, 2 : 212.

(Davis, H.) Shakspere and John Lyly. Poet Lore 5 : 177 (Ap.'93).

(Davis, L. Clarke.) "These our Actors." (Daly's Co.) Lippinc. 32 : 369.

> Among the Comedians. Atlan. 19 : 750.

> Drama in Tatters. Chamb. J. 60 : 215.

> Joseph Jefferson as Rip Van Winkle. Lippinc. 24 : 57 (Jl.'59).

> John E. Owens. Atlan. 19 : 750.

> Actors, Old and New. Galaxy 15 : 660.

(**Davis**, L. Clarke.) Drama in Philadelphia. Amer. 3: 55.
Maggie Mitchell and Mary Gannon. Galaxy 6: 245.
Jefferson as Rip Van Winkle. Atlan. 19: 750.

(**Davis**, Richard Harding.) Mrs. Kendal vs. American Public.
The. n. s. 23: 9 (F.'94) (reprint from Harper's
Weekly).

Deadheads, What to do With. (A. Patterson) The. 27 n. s.
'80 (F.'96).
Should they live? (H. C. Newton) The. n. s. 28: 147
(S.'96).

(**Deane**, A. C.) Stage in Fiction. The. n. s. 11: 104 (S.'92).

Dearth of Dramatists. Theatre '80, 1: 1.

Deaths, Sudden, of Actors. (S. W. Clarke) The. n. s. 10:
75.
Deaths and Disasters on the Stage. Chamb. J. 53: 13.

(**De Brémont**, A.) American Actresses. The. 18: 324.

Decay of the Stage. St. Paul's 1: 173. Same art. Ecl. M.
70: 54.

(**De Colonne**, Vicomte.) Drama in France. Macmil. 34: 176.

(**De Cordova**, Rudolph.) The Stage as a Career. Forum 17:
622 (Jl.'94).

(**de Dubor**, George.) Plays of Hroswitha. Fortn. 65: 443
(Mr.'96).

(**De Falbe**, Count.) The Hamlet Saga. 19th Cent. 12: 147
(D.'82).
Hamlet, Where he came from. Manhat. 1: 132.

(**De Gibbins**, H.) Björnsterne Björnson. To-day 10: 43.

De Grey, Marie. The. '81, 2: 129.

(**De Kay**, Chas.) Modjeska. Scrib. 17: 665 (Mr.'79).

(**De la Barca**, Mme. C.) The Drama. No. Am. 39: 335.

(**De la Ramée**, L.) *See "Ouida."*

Delaunay, as an Actor. Sat. R. 63: 725.

(**De Leon**, T. C.) Christmas Pantomimes. Lippinc. 3 : 36.

(**DeLong**, M. J.) Faust Legend. Univ. R. 46 : 208.

Delsarte. (F. A. Duvivage) Atlan. 27 : 613.

De Maupassant, Guy, as a Dramatist. (C. Nicholson) Acad.
    39 : 265.

(**De Meusiaux**, M.) "A Fool's Paradise," "Snowball."
    See "Sydney Grundy."
    Wilson Barrett in "The Golden Ladder."

"**Denise.**" *See "Dumas, fils."*

(**Dennett**, J. R.) Theatres of Our Day. Nation 7 : 500.
    Shakspere's Delineation of Insanity. Nation 2 : 758.

Desdemona. Am. Mo. M. 7 : 209. (D. Fowler) Canad.
    Mo. 19 : 643. (H. F. Martin) Blackw. 129 : 325.
    (Mr. '81). Same art. Ecl. M. 96 : 643. Same art.
    Appleton 25 : 399. Same art. Liv. Age 149 : 206. *See
    also " Othello."*

(**De Wolfe**, E. A.) Women of the Comédie Française. Cos-
    mop. 11 : 643.

(**Dicey**, A. V.) R. B. Sheridan. Nation 39 : 136.

Dickens, Chas., Amateur Theatricals of. Macmil 23 : 206.
    Same art. Ecl. M. 76 : 322; also Ev. Sat. 10 : 70.
    and the Play. (G. Turner) The. '85, 1 : 171.
    as a Dramatic Critic. (D. Cook) Longm. 2 : 29.
    as a Dramatist. Spec. 55 : 953. Same art. Liv. Age
    154 : 362.
    as a Dramatist and Poet. (P. Fitzgerald) Gent. M. n. s.
    20 : 61.
    on the American Stage. (G. E. Montgomery) No. Am.
    8 : 190.

(**Dickens**, Chas., 2d.) Censorship. The. n. s. 25 : 10 (Ja.'95).
    Decadence of Pantomime. The. n. s. 27 : 21 (Ja.'96).
    Difficulties of the Serious Drama. The. n. s. 27 : 200
    (Ap.'96).
    Fechter's Acting. Atlan. 24 : 242.

(**Donne**, W. B.) Dramatic Representation.   Dark Blue
1: 70.

Ward on English Dramatic Literature. Macmil. 33: 314.

(**Donnely**, T.) Drury Lane. Godey 128: 341 (Mr.'94).

Don Quixote on the Stage.   (A. Escott) The. n. s. 25: 267
(My.'95).

(**Doran**, Dr.) Shakspere in France. 19th Cent. 3: 115
(Ja.'78).

(**Doran** J.) French Criticisms on Shakspere. 19th Cent.
3: 115. Same art. Liv. Age 136: 533.

Doran's Annals of the Stage. Dub. Univ. 63: 155.

(**Dorchester**, D., Jr.) "Hamlet." Meth. R. 52: 390 (My. &
Je.'92).

(**Dorr**, J. C. R.) Caroline Howard Gilman. Critic 13: 151.

(**Douglas**, B. K.) Chinese Drama. Contemp. 37: 123.
Same art. Ecl. M. 94: 349.

(**Dowden**, Edward.) Shakspere's Wisdom of Life. Fortn.
50: 405. Same art. Ecl. M. 111: 668. Liv. Age
179: 131.

Kemble's Notes on Shakspere. Acad. 22: 409.

Shakspere's Historical Plays. Acad. 23: 90.

Some Books on Shakspere. Acad. 28: 127.

Women of Shakspere. Contemp. 47: 517. Same art.
Liv. Age 165: 405.

(**Downes**, H.) One Night on the Stage. Once a Week 1:
295, 317.

Drama, Scrib. 21: 632 (F.'81). (C. de la Barca) No. Am.
39: 335. (J. R. Lowell) No. Am. 66: 374, 400. (W.
B. O. Peabody) No. Am. 31: 445. (H. Ware, Jr.)
No. Am. 45: 313, 335.

a Course of Reading on the. (J. B. Matthews) Critic 3:
215.

Ancient, and the Modern Novel. (K. Cook) Dark Blue
3 : 709.

and Music. Blackw. 6: 430. Irish Mo. 9: 104.

Drama and Music Halls. Cornh. 15: 119.

 as it is. (J. H. McCarthy) Gent. M. n. s. 49: 533 (N. '92).

 Character and Tendencies of. Ed. R. 90: 129.

 Classic, 1858–67. Ch. R. 55: 39.

 Classic and Romantic. Putnam's 6: 401. For. Quar. R. 36: 42.

 Conventionalities of. (F. Parke) Dub. Univ. 85: 503.

 Decadent. (Edw. Fuller) Lippinc. 56: 423 (S. '95).

 (D. Boucicault) No. Am. 125: 235. (H. Quilter) Contemp. 5: 547. Same art. Ecl. M. 108: 824.

 Decadence of. Tait 2: 380.

 Decline of. (D. Boucicault) No. Am. 125: 235. (J. B. Matthews) Galaxy 19: 225. Chamb. J. 38: 392. Tait n. s. 18: 600. Tinsley 5: 293. (S. Grundy) The. n. s. 27: 131 (Mr.'96). 27: 196 (Ap. '96).

 Deterioration of. (Morris Ross) Poet Lore 3: 353 (Jl.'91).

 Dialogue on. (A. H. Kennedy) 19th Cent. 38: 322 (Ag.'95).

 Domestics of the. (W. Gordon) The.'81, 2: 19.

 Drunken. (O. Logan) Galaxy 4: 934. (C. Reade) Spec. 55: 1079.

 Dying. (W. Archer) New R. 1: 367. Poet Lore 1: 527 (N.'89).

 The Eternal Truths of the. (Mme. Fanny Janauschek.) Dr. Mirror, 35: 886 (Xmas '95).

 Epitome of. (R. Lee) The. '86, 2: 258.

 Footlights of Other Days. Tinsley 10: 465.

 For and Against. (J. Pollock) 19th Cent. 1: 611.

 French Opinions of. (C. Bonjour) Colburn 53: 363.

 Girardin on. For Quar. R. 33: 33. Same art. Ecl. M. 3: 33.

 Habitué's Note Book. (C. Hervey) Colburn 84: 122, 535; 85: 125, 502; 86: 113, 383; 87: 373, 490; 88: 123, 550; 89: 129, 381; 90: 116, 244.

 Hazlitt's Lecture on. (T. N. Talfourd) Ed. R. 34: 438.

 Historical. Once a Week 28: 170.

7

Drama under Difficulty.　All the Year 36: 102.　Chamb. J.
　26: 289.

　Vicissitudes of.　(L. Barrett) No. Am. 146: 203.

　Will, Live?　(Wm. Gillette) Dr. Mirror, 23: 578 (Jan. 25,
　'90).

Dramas, Stage Right to.　Sat. R. 59: 208.

Dramatic Art, Four Centuries of.　(E. W. L.) Lippinc. 27:
　522 (My.'81).

　and Theatrical, Differences of.　(F. A. Kemble) Cornh.
　8: 733.

　Art, School of.　*See "School," etc.*

　Art of the Present Day.　(D. M. Craik) 19th Cent. 20:
　416.

　Art, Past and Present.　Dub. Univ. 73: 511.

　Art, Influence of Theatre on.　Lon. M. 1: 146.

　Art.　(J. Pollock) Contemp. 23: 363.

　Author and the Dramatic Critic, The.　(Brander Mat-
　thews) Dr. Mirror, 23: 574 (D. 28, '89).

　Difficulties.　All the Year 73: 135 (Ag. 5, '93).

　Doing.　Dub. Univ. 16: 641 ; 17: 328, 599; 18: 180;
　19: 64.

　Doctors.　All the Year 39: 373.

　Emancipation.　Putnam 2: 369.

　in the Far East.　(R. W. E. Eastlake) Chamb. J. 72: 251
　(Ja. '95).

　Opinions.　(Mrs. Kendal) Murray 6: 289, 733.

　Outlook, 1885.　(H. A. Jones) Eng. Illust. 2: 280, 341.

　Ring.　(Sydney Grundy) The.'79, 2: 273.

　Representation.　(W. B. Donne) Dark Blue 1: 70.

　Sensation.　(W. P. Wood) Lakeside 9: 9.

Dramatic License.　(W. G. Wills) The. '80, 1: 199.

Dramatiques, Proverbes.　(T. Le Clerq) Lon. M. 12: 17.

Dramatist, My Début and Early Days as a.　(D. Boucicault)
　No. Am. 148: 454 (Ap. '89).　148: 584 (My.'89).

Dramatist, Leaves from the Diary of a.   (D. Boucicault) No.
Am. 149 : 228 (Ag. '89).
A Dead : a Dialogue. The. 28 : 80 (F.'92).
Discontents of a.   (H. C. Wilson) The.'86, 1 : 175.
Grievances of.   The.'79, 1 : 71.

Dramatists, Competent.   The.'79, 1 : 1.
Doctors and.   (W. E. McCann) Dr. Mirror 23 : 597
(Je. 7,'90).
Foreign, Under American Laws.   (E. S. Drone) Scrib.
9 : 90 (N.'75).
Grievances of.   The.'79, 1 : 71.
Modern.   Tinsley 6 : 421.
Women as.   All the Year 75 : 296 (S. 29,'94).
Dearth of.   The.'80, 1 : 1.

Dresses, Stage, of the Month.   (Mrs. Armstrong) The. n. s.
24 : 61 (Ag.'94).

(Drew, John.) The Actor.   Scribner 15 : 32 (Ja.'94).

(Drone, F. S.) Foreign Dramatists Under American Laws.
Scrib. 9 : 90 (N. '75).

Drunkenness on the Stage. (Alphonse Daudet) The. n. s.
24 : 48 (Ag.'94).

Drury Lane.   (J. Coleman) Gent. M. n. s. 57 : 365 (O. '96).
(V. Gribayédoff and T. Donnely.) Godey 128 : 341 (Mr.
'94).
Old.   Harper 22 : 126 (D.'60).   Temp. Bar 13 : 443.

Drury Lane Theatre.   (A. Harris) Fortn. 45 : 650. All the
Year 42 : 346.
in Time of James I. (J. Greenstreet) Ath.'85, 2 : 59, 282.
Behind Scenes at.   All the Year 66 : 302.
Managers from Killegrew to Harris.   (P. H. Fitzgerald)
The. n. s. 9 : 25, 295.

Duels, Stage.   Sat. R. 71 : 582.

Duff, Mary Dyke.   (G. W. Allen) Amer. 4 : 170.

Dumas, Alex., *père*.   Dramas of.   (J. B. Matthews) 48 : 383.
Dramatic Genius of.   Knick. 3 : 190.
" Francillon."   (A. Langel) Nation 44 : 139.
Modern Republican Tragedy.   Fraser 39 : 188.
Theatrical Experience of.   Dub. Univ. 77 : 241.

Dumas *fils*.   Bentley 41 : 347.   Lond. Soc. 25 : 208.   Same
art. Ecl. M. 82 : 613.   (F. Belmore) Tinsley 35 : 35.
(A. Cohns) Bkm. (Ja.'96).   (R. Davey) The. n. s.
27 : 12 (Ja. '96).   (J. B. Fletcher) Harv. Mo. 13 : 1.
(H. James) New R. (Mr. '96), Temp. Bar 51 : 392.
(L. H. Hooper) Lippinc. 21 : 501 (Ap. '78).   (J. B.
Matthews) Internat. 10 : 503.   (Mme. van de Velde)
Fortn. (Ja. '96).
and Eng. Drama.   (W. Archer) Cosmop. 1 : 363 (F. '96).
at Home.   Lit. World (Boston) 24 : 176 (Ja. 3, '93).
" Camille."   Three Ladies of the Camelias : Duse, Bern-
hardt, and Nethersole.   (B. Fletcher) Godey 132 : 477
(Je. '96).
" La Dame aux Camélias."   Sat. R. 53 : 426.
" Denise."   (A. Langel) Nation 40 : 136. Sat. R. 59 : 210.
" Diane de Lys," at the Princess's Theatre.   St. Paul's
13 : 211.

Du Maurier, George.   " Trilby " as a Play.   (B. Fletcher) Godey
130 : 570 (Je. '95).

(Dunlap, Wm.)   Fraser 7 : 436.
Geo. Fredk. Cooke.   Anal. M. 1 : 404, 466.

(Durivage, F. A.)   Delsarte.   Atlan. 27 : 613.

Duse, Eleanora.   Sat. R. 75 : 571 (My. 27, '93).   Ath. '85,
1 : 673.   (W. Archer) Fortn. 64 : 299 (Ag. '95).   (Blackburn) New R. 13 : 39 (Jl. '95).   (P. Schleuther)
Looker On (Mr. '96).   (M. C. Jones) Critic 22 : 67,
117 (F. 4, 25, '93).   (J. R. Towse) Cent. 51 : 130
(N. '95).
as Camille.   (P. Houghton) The. n. s. 23 : 303 (Je.'94).
in " Cavalleria Rusticana," and " La Locandiera."   (Philip
Houghton) The. n. s. 24 : 27 (Jl. '94).

Duse, Terry, and Bernhardt. (Maud Andrews) New Bohemian
2 : 184 (My. '96).

Duty of the Church as to the Theatre. (N. Hall; H. C.
Shuttleworth) Ch. Lit. 11 : 302 (S. '94).

(Dyer, J.) Church and the Theatre. Penn Mo. 10 : 374.

(Dyer, L.) Greek Play at Bradfield College, 1892. Nation
55 : 26 (Jl. 14,'92).

(Dyer, T. F. T.) Out-door Plays. Art. J. 37 : 301.

Eastlake, Mary. With portrait. The. '83, 1 : 310.
in " Hoodman Blind." The. '85, 2 : 291, 342.

(Eastwick, R. W. E.) Dramatic Art in Far East. Chamb.
J. 72 : 251 (Ja. '95).

(Edgarton, H. E.) Historical Drama. National 17 : 743.

(Edgarton, Robt.) Marie Burroughs. Lippinc. 51 : 363
(Mr. '93).

Edgeworth, Maria. Comic Dramas. Quart. 17 : 96. Mo.
R. 83 : 315.

Education. Education of an Actor. (D. Boucicault) No.
Am. 147 : 435.
Stage as an Educator. Harper 79 : 474 (Ag. '89). (J.
P. Walton) Westm. 142 : 567 (N. '94).
(W. O. Partridge) Am. J. Soc. Sci. 21 : 188.

(Edwards, C.) Hamlet a Fat Man. Contin Mo. 1 : 571
(My. '62).
Shylock vs. Antonio. Contin. Mo. 3 : 539.

(Edwards, E. J.) Oratory: Is it a Lost Art? Chaut. 14 : 445
(Ja. '92).

(Edwards, H. Southerland). Drama in Russia. The. n. s.
26 : 213 (O. '95).
Stage Anomalies. Macmil. 41 : 322. Same art. Appleton
23 : 358.

(Egan, M. F.) " Becket." Cath. World 43 : 382.

(Egan, P.) Minor Theatres of London. Atlan. 25 : 294.

(**Elliott**, Henry.)   Royalty and Theatre Closing.   The. n. s.
27: 154 (Mr. '96).
Suburban Theatre.   The. n. s. 26: 273 (N. '95).
Fanciful Comedy.   The. n. s. 28: 77 (Ag. '96).

(**Elliott**, W. G.)   Amateur Acting.   National 24: 628 (Ja. '95).

(**Ellis**, Leanora Beck.)   A Tale of Modern Chivalry: "Prisoner
of Zenda."   Illust. (Je. and Jl. '96).

(**Ellis**, R.)   Passion Play at Ober Ammergau.   Mo. Rel. M.
44: 209.

Elliston, R. W.   Manager Drury Lane.   Lon. M. 1: 69.
Temp. Bar 48: 315.

Elliston and Wallack.   (J. H. Liddons) Harper 25: 73
(Je. '62).

Ellistoniana.   (W. T. Moncrieff) Colburn 67: 22, 532; 68: 99,
529; 69: 129, 557.

Elizabeth, Queen, Shakspere, Falstaff and.   19th Cent. (F.
'96).

Elizabethan Stage, The.   (W. Poel) The. n. s. 22: 241
(N. '93).

Elizabethan Theatre.   (W. A. Leahy) Harv. Mo. 6: 207.

Elocution.   "How Can I Become a Distinct Speaker?"   (R.
M. Cumnoch) Chaut. 10: 320.
Ministerial Tone.   (R. M. Cumnoch) Chaut. 13: 53.

Elocutionist, My Experience as an.   (Cora Urquhart Potter)
Lippinc. 37: 534 (My. '86).

Elssler, Fanny, and the Tarantella.   So. Lit. Mess. 6: 700.
in London, Paris, and Havanah.   Fraser 28: 713; 29: 78,
144, 274.

(**Elze**, K.)   "King Edward II."   Ath. '87, 1: 491.

(**Emerson**, O. F.)   "Antony and Cleopatra."   Poet Lore 2: 71,
125, 188.

Emery, Winifred.   The. n. s. 22: 196 (O. '93).   (W. A. L.
Bettany) The. n. s. 22: 301 (D. '93).
With portrait.   The. n. s. 24: 282 (D. '94).

Emotional Expression. (A. T. Bruce) Am. Natural. 17 : 613.

Emotionalism. Archer's "Masks and Faces." Sat. R. 66 : 606 (N. 24, '88).
Archer's "Psychology." Ath. '89, 1 : 156.
Diderot's "Paradoxe." Westm. 127 : 44. (N. Hapgood) Harv. Mo. 9 : 7.
Mr. Irving on the Art of Acting. ("Ouida") 19th Cent. 37 : 786 (My. '95).

Empty Benches. Chamb. J. 67 : 830.

Endowed Theatres and the American Stage. (Helena Modjeska) Forum 14 : 337 (N. '92).

English Acting in '95. The. n. s. 27 : 63 (F. '96).

English Actors. His Majesty's Servants. (C. B. L. Woodburne) Gent. M. n. s. 51 : 60 (Jl. '93).
Actors and Actresses. Temple Bar 11 : 135.
in Paris. Colburn 5 : 259.

English Actresses, Early. Fraser 31 : 673.

English Drama. (A. H. Everett) No. Am. 38 : 172. (A. B. Walkley) Cosmopolis 1 : 88 (Ja.'96). Quart. 132 : 1. Blackw. 14 : 421, 723; 18 : 119. Blackw. 89 : 218; Mo. R. 150 : 457; 151 : 291; 152 : 347. Dub. Univ. 28 : 525, 668. Amer. 12 : 8.
in '94 and '95. Sat. R. 80 : 107 (Jl. 27, '95).
During Commonwealth. (W. H. Hudson) The. n. s. 10 : 177.
Early. (W. H. Withrow) Meth. R. 54 : 534. Retros. 2 : 70; 3 : 97, 142; 16 : 1.
and German. (W. J. Thoms) Colburn 61 : 19.
Future of. (H. A. Jones) Univ. R. 9 : 177 (Ag. '93).
Lamb's Specimens. Ath. '94, 2 : 265 (Ag. 25, '94).
Stage Conditions of. (W. A. Leahy) Harv. Mo. 6 : 207.
Stage of Greater Britain. National 6 : 401 (N. '85).
Anglo-French Drama. Ed. R. 51 : 119.
Dawn of. National Q. 28 : 97.

8

English Drama, Decline of. Cornh. 8 : 172. Colburn 153 :
    304. Blackw. 23 : 33; Mus. 12 : 661. Sharpe. 39 :
    6, 231 ; 40 : 187, 230, 287 ; 41 : 18.
    and French. Macmil. 20 : 70. Same art. Ecl. M. 73 : 87.
    in Time of Elizabeth and James. Cornh. 11 : 604, 706;
    12 : 86.
    in 1853. Quart. 95 : 71.
    in 1873. Dub. Univ. 82 : 240, 492.
    Modern. Blackw. 72 : 209. Dub. R. 2 : 367. No.
    Brit. 29 : 124. Same art. Ecl. M. 46 : 29.
    Notes on. So. Lit. Mess. 4 : 533.
    Old. Retros. 2 : 70 ; 3 : 97, 142 ; 11 : 123 ; Mo. R.
    111 : 365 ; 109 : 388.
    State of. Victoria 28 : 520.
    of To-day. (H. Merivale) Temp. Bar 77 : 371. Same
    art. Ecl. M. 107 : 283.
    See also " London Drama."

English Dramatic Poetry. Quart. 46 : 477.

English Dramatists, Old, Lowell on. Lippinc. 70 : 524
    (Ap. 22, '93).
    Dramatists, Old English. (E. P. Whipple) No. Am.
    63 : 29. So. Lit. Mess. 15 : 656. Westm. 1 : 560.

English Players in Paris. (W. J. Lawrence) Gent. M. n. s.
    45 : 446.

English Playgoer. Tinsley 3 : 634.

English Plays on Foreign Stages. All the Year 62 : 19.

English Stage and the Comédie Française. Dub. Univ. 94 : 340.

English Stage in 19th Century. (J. H. Siddons) Potter's
    Am. Mo. 18 : 565, 639 ; 19 : 14, 139, 245.

English Theatre in 18th Century. (J. Picciotto) Dub. Univ.
    77 : 703.
    Shortcomings of. (T. Taylor) Dark Blue 1 : 746.
    Dub. Univ. 28 : 525, 668.

English Tragedy. Ed. R. 38 : 177.

(Errington, J.) " Merchant of Venice." M. 61 : 393.

(Escott, Arthur.) The Claque. The. n. s. 27: 256 (My.'96).
Don Quixote on the Stage. The. n. s. 25: 267 (My. '95).
Felons on the Stage. The. n. s. 28: 150 (S. '96).
John Hall. The. n. s. 26: 333 (D. '95).
Mrs. Stirling. The. n. s. 27: 86 (F. '96).
T. W. Robertson. The. n. s. 26: 29 (Jl. '95).

Esmond, Georgia. The. n. s. 20: 112 (S.'92).

(Esmond, Georgia.) Henry V. The. n. s. 19: 198 (Ag. '92).
The. 27: 36 (Ja. '96).

(Evans, E. P.) Shakspere: Player and Poet. Lakeside
2: 173.

(Everett, A. H.) Goeffry on Dramatic Literature. No.
Am. 10: 291.
English Drama. No. Am. 38: 172.
Spanish Drama. No. Am. 38: 166.

(Everett, E.) Hindu Drama. No. Am. 26: 111.

(Everts, Julie M.) Study of Acting in Paris. Cent. 6: 471 (Jl.'84.)

Expression, Dramatic. (A. W. Robbins) Lippinc. 53: 242
(F.'94).

Extravaganza and Spectacle on the Stage. (J. R. Planché)
Temp. Bar 3: 524.

(Fairholt, F. W.) At a Pantomime. St. James 3: 193.

"Faded Flower." History of a Single Act Play (A. W.
a Beckett) The. n. s. 25: 204 (Ap.'95).

(Faithful, E.) Duty of an Audience. The. '79, 2: 76.

(Falconer, E.) Hamlet. The. '79, 1: 171.

False Emphasis. (W. H. Pollock) The. n. s. 26: 85 (Ag. '95).

Falstaff, Sir John, Character of. Sat. R. 56: 597; 64: 748;
So. M. 15: 214; Westm. 6: 370. Liv. Age 63: 614.
Domestic Character of. Lon. M. 1: 194. (J. G. Kelly)
Overland 13: 352.
Hackett's. Harper 35: 394 (Ag.'67).
Shakspere's, the Original of. (W. J. Fitzpatrick) Gent.
M. n. s. 38: 428.

Falstaff, Sir John, Historic Element in.   (J. Gardnice) Fortn.
19: 333.
"King Henry IV," and, on the Stage.   (F. Hawkins)
The. n. s. 27: 211 (Ap.'96).
Shakspere, and Queen Elizabeth. 19th Cent. (F. '96).
Was he Immoral? (L. D. Lawhead) Poet Lore 2: 142.

Falstaff's Deathbed. (C. Creighton) Blackw. 145: 324.

Falstaffs, Famous. (R. W. Lowe) The. 22: 185.
Stage. (W. J. Lawrence) Gent. M. n. s. 42: 425.
Unknown to Fame. The. 22: 257.

Farren, Eliz. (L. Wingfield) The. '80, 1: 319.

Farren, W. The. '78, 2: 360.

(Farren W.) Insanity of Hamlet. Lon. M. 9: 373, 647.
Madness of King Lear. Lon. M. 10: 79.

Faust. (I. Tourgénieff) Fortn. 62: 729 (Jl.'94).
and Mephistopheles. (W. D. Conway) Harper 38: 541
(Mr.'69).
as a Puppet Show. Cornh. 47: 92.
on English Stage. (J. Hatton) Art J. 38: 57, 88. (W.
D. Courtney) Fortn. 45: 102. (W. H. Pollock) National 6: 833.
The Stage. (W. S. Sichel) National 6: 211 (O.'85).
Wills', at the Lyceum. (F. A. Marshall) The. '86, 1: 59.

(Fawcett, E.) Literature and the Drama. Dial (Ch.) 14: 38.
Spanish-American Burlesque. Lakeside 4: 190.

Fawcett, John. Colburn 51: 316.

Fechter, Chas. Albert. (K. Field) Atlan. 26: 285.   (D.
Cook) The. '79, 2: 132. Lit. World (Bost.) 13: 309.
Sat. R. 55: 237. Harper 24: 562 (Mr.'62); 41:
295 (Jl.'70). (G. B. Woods) O. and N. 1: 514.
Cornh. 8: 171. Galaxy 9: 554.
Acting of. (C. Dickens) Atlan. 24: 242. Ev. Sat. 10:
138.
Green Room Recollections of. (A. W. a Beckett) The.
n. s. 24: 116 (S.'94).

First Night, One's, at the Play. (F. Jacox) Colburn 142 : 35.
    Same art. Liv. Age 96 : 735.

First Nights at the Play. Dub. Univ. 90 : 226.

First Nights of Famous Plays. Chamb. J. 68 : 601 (S. 19,
    '91).
    in London Theatres. (C. E. Pascoe) Amer. 1 : 103.

(Fiske, Mrs. Minnie Maddern.) Tricks of the Trade. Dr.
    Mirror, 23 : 589 (Ap. 12,'90).

(Fiske, Stephen.) Actor-Management.   Dr. Mirror 24 : 601
    (Jl. 5, '90).
    A Note on Dion Boucicault. The. n. s. 24 : 301 (D. '94).
    The Irving Influence in America. The. n. s. 27 : 158.
    Playwriting Critics. Dr. Mirror, 23 : 583 (M. 1, '90).

(Fitch, A. S.) Henry Irving and his Work. Manhat. 2 :
    391.

(Fitch, Geo. H.) In a Chinese Theatre. Cent. 2 : 189 (Je. '82).

Fitzgerald, Edw. Letters to Fanny Kemble. Temple Bar
    104 : 27, 473; 105 : 33, 486 (Ja., Ag. '95). (R. C.
    Browne) Acad. 48 : 451 (N. 30, '95). (W. Garrison)
    Nation 61 : 297 (O. 24, '95). (W. G. Johnson) Dial
    (Ch.) 19 : 174 (O. 1, '95).

Fitzgerald, Percy. Memoirs of. Sat. R. 79 : 679 (My. 25,
    '95).

(Fitzgerald, Percy.) Daly's Company in "Taming of the
    Shrew." The. 21 : 10.
    Dickens as a Dramatist and Poet. Gent. M. n. s. 20 : 61.
    Faces of Actors. The. '78, 2 : 354.
    Garrick Club Portraits. Gent. M. n. s. 18 : 561.
    Life of Garrick. See " Garrick."
    "Hamlet " with Alterations. The. '86, 1 : 252.
    Construction and Arrangement of Theatres. Art J. 28 :
        13, 357.
    Grand Theatres and Opera Houses. The. n. s. 24 : 111
        (S. '94).

(Fitzgerald, Percy.) Romance of English Stage. Lippinc. 15: 518 (Ap. '75).

Behind the Scenes at the Lyceum. Belgra. 44: 335.

Social Position of the Actor in England. The. n. s. 26: 6 (Jl. '96).

Chronicles of the Stage. Month 42: 71, 535; 43: 81, 507.

(Fitzgerald, Percy and P. H.) On Some of the Old Actors. Gent. M. n. s. 52: 82, 70 (Ja. & F. '94).

Confessions of an Old Æsthete. The. '82, 1: 8.

Geo. Coleman and D. Garrick. The. 18: 340.

First Appearance of David Garrick. The. '82, 1: 308.

Managers of Drury Lane. The. 18: 28, 295.

Humors of W. S. Gilbert. The. '81, 2: 339.

Religion of Hamlet. Month 53: 64. Same art. Liv. Age 164: 461.

First Appearance of John and Fanny Kemble. The. '86, 2: 117.

Mrs. Langtry as Pauline. The. '86, 1: 221.

London Music Halls. National 15: 379.

Sir Edw. B. Lytton's "Lady of Lyons." Gent. M. n. s. 43: 136.

Origin and Development of the Play Bill. Gent. M. n. s. 40: 373.

Daly's Company in "Railroad of Love." The. 20: 315.

R. B. Sheridan's "School for Scandal." The. '82, 1: 171.

Fitz-Gerald, S. J. A. The. n. s. 27: 29 (Ja. '96).

(Fitz-Gerald, S. J. A.) Play Bills Old and New. The. n. s. 15: 292.

Influence of Criticism. The. n. s. 24: 238 (N. '94).

Lyric Drama and Libretti. The. 29: 161 (O. '92).

(Fitzpatrick, W. J.) Original of Shakspere's Falstaff. Gent. M. n. s. 38: 428.

(Fleming, A.) Behind the Scenes. Harper 34: 114 (D. '66).

(Fleay, F. G.) Who Wrote Our Old Plays? Macmil. 30: 408.

Lists of Actors 1578–1642. Roy. Hist. Soc. 9: 44.

Text of Shakspere. Macmil. 36: 195.

Shakspere's Stage Life. Poet Lore 5: 7–612 (J.–D.' 93).

Fleay's History of London Stage. Poet Lore 3: 149 (Mr. '91).

(Fletcher, Beaumont.) "Chimmie Fadden." Godey 132: 361 (Ap. '96).

Duse, Bernhardt, and Nethersole as Camille. Godey 132: 477 (My. '96).

"Christopher, Jr." Godey 132: 19 (Ja. '96).

Frank Daniels in "Wizard of the Nile." Godey 132: 234 (Mr. '96).

"The Heart of Maryland." Godey 132: 180 (F. '96).

Frank Mayo as Pudd'nhead Wilson. Godey 131: 8 (Jl. '95).

Mrs. Potter. Godey 131: 476 (N. '95).

The Stage and the Church. Godey 131: 280 (S. '95).

Julia Marlowe Taber. Godey 132: 589 (Je. '96).

"Trilby" as a Play. Godey 130: 570 (Je. '95).

Walker Whiteside as Hamlet. Godey 131: 624 (D. '95).

Russ Whytal's "For Fair Virginia." Godey 131: 127 (Ag. '95).

(Fletcher, G.) Criticism and Acting of Macbeth. Westm. 41: 1.

"Merchant of Venice." Fraser 41: 499, 697.

(Fletcher, J. B.). Dumas, *fils.* Harv. Mo. 13: 1.

Florence, Theatres in. (C. Hervey) The. '85, 2: 35.

Florence, Wm. Jermyn. Critic 19: 307. The. '81, 2: 191, 222.

Fools. *See "Buffoons," etc.*

(Ford, Jas. L.) The Independent or Free Theatre of New York. Lippinc. 49: 375 (Mr. '92).

(**Ford,** Paul Leicester.) Beginnings of American Dramatic Literature. N. Eng. M. n. s. 9: 673 (F. '94).

"**Formosa.**" *See "Boucicault."*

Forrest, Edwin. Harper 4: 563; 28: 131 (?) (Je. '63).
(L. Barrett) Cent. 2: 468. (L. Barrett) Galaxy 24: 256. (A. E. Lancaster) Potter Am. Mo. 8: 161. Am. Bibliop. 4: 634. Knick. 11: 85.
Alger's Life of. (J. B. Matthews) Nation 25: 124.
in England. Dem. R. 16: 385; 19: 186.
and Macready. (S. Osgood) Harper 47: 298 (Jl. '73).
Oration of. Dem. R. 3: 51.
Reminiscences of. Potter Am. Mo. 12: 369.

Forsyth, Helen. The. '86, 1: 291, 341.

Fortescue, Miss. (H. Aspden) The. n. s. 22: 181 (O. '93).

Foster, C. S., and Negro Minstrelsy. (R. P. Nevin) Atlan. 20: 608.

(**Foster,** J.) Plumptre on the Stage. Ecl. R. 10: 1031.
History of Theatrical Amusements. Ecl. R. 10: 1031.

(**Fowler,** D.) Desdemona. Canad. Mo. 19: 643.
Ophelia and Portia. Canad. Mo. 19: 504.

(**Fox,** H. J.) Genius and Times of Shakspere. Meth. Q. 41: 623.

(**Fox,** W. J.) W. C. Macready. Peop. J. 2: 323, 347.

Foyers of Paris Theatres. Vaudeville. (C. Hervey) The. '82, 1: 265.
Variétés. (C. Hervey) The. '81, 2: 283.
Boulevard. (C. Hervey) The. '83, 1: 137.
Gymnase. (C. Hervey) The. '82, 2: 153.
Italien and Odéon. (C. Hervey) The. '84, 2: 219.
Minor. (C. Hervey) The. '85, 1: 63.

(**Francis,** L. E.) Uncanny Characters of Shakspere. Educa. 11: 293.

(**Franklyn,** C. W.) Shakspere. Westm. 13: 348.

9

(Frazer, J. G.) Slavonic Parallel to "Merchant of Venice."
Acad. 27: 330.

Free List Vagaries. The. n. s. 23: 64 (F. '94).

French Actors, Comic. Colburn 6: 341; 8: 341.
Early, Notes on. Colburn 53: 15.
in the Green Room. Colburn 4: 309.

French Actors and Actresses. (C. Hervey) Colburn 83: 577.
Old. All the Year, 38: 173, 413; 39: 160, 489; 40: 183: 541.

French Actresses. Ev. Sat. 15: 485.
A Line of. Temp. Bar 39: 369.

French Comedy. (J. Pollock) Contemp. 18: 43. (F. Sarcey)
19th Cent. 6: 182; Quart. 29: 414. Westm. 31: 69.
Cornh. 40: 50.
after Molière's Day. Dub. Univ. 75: 125.
and Comedians in. Bentley 47: 368.

French Drama. (W. Sargent) No. Am. 78: 319. (A. R.
Spofford) No. Am. 81: 336. (A. Langel) Nation
34: 51. (Vicomte de Colonne) Macmil. 34: 176.
Lon. 2d. s. 5: 44. For. Quar. Rev. 4: 309; 9: 78; 31:
140. Quart. 51: 177. (G. H. Lewes) Westm. 34: 287.
Cornh. 11: 33. Dem. R. 21: 333. New R. 10: 127.
(J. Pollock) Contemp. 21: 335. Putnam 6: 401.
In 1820. (J. B. Matthews) Amer. 1: 124.
Present Tendencies of. (J. B. Matthews) Lippinc.
27: 383.
Shakspere in France. (Dr. Doran) 19th Cent. 3: 115
(Ja. '78).
of To-day. (W. M. Fullerton) The. n. s. 25: 81 (F.'95).
under Louis XIV. (H. M. Trollope) Macmil. 31: 522.
in London. (M. Arnold) 19th Cent. 6: 228. Same art.
Appleton 22: 311. (F. and W. H. Pollock) Dark
Blue 2: 102.
in 1875. Dub. Univ. 85: 204, 379, 743. Quart. 139: 138.
in 1876. Dub. Univ. 87: 108.
in 16th Century. Retros. 18: 396.
Modern. (E. I. Sears) Nat. Q. 1: 64.

French Tragedy.   (R. G. White) Atlan. 47: 827.   Quart.
   29: 25.
   Before Corneille.   (G. Saintsbury.)   Fraser 100: 456.
   Tragic Drama.   Corneille.   Nat. Q. 23: 256.

Freytag, Gustav.   On the Technique of the Drama.   (J. S.
   Mollen) Dial (Ch.) 18: 77.

(Frost, H. W.)   The Stage as it Was.   Galaxy 16: 483, 599.

(Frothingham, O. B.)   Worship of Shakspere.   Cent. 7:
   780.
   Acting of Edwin Booth.   Nation 2: 395.
   Theatres.   Nation 2: 428.

Frou-Frou.   Authors of the Play.   (J. B. Matthews) Lippinc.
   26: 711.

(Fryers, A.)   Aristotle's Definition of Tragedy.   The. 26: 227.

(Fuller, Edw.)   The Decadent Drama.   Lippinc. 56: 423
   (S. '95).
   An Independent Theatre.   Lippinc. 49: 371 (Mr. '92).
   The Public and the Theatre.   Lippinc. 46: 564 (O. '90).
   The Theatrical Renaissance of Shakspere.   Lippinc.
   45: 38 (J. '90).

(Fullerton, H. Morton.)   French Drama of To-day.   The. n. s.
   25: 81 (F. '95).

(Furnivall, F. J.)   Hamlet's "Sea of Troubles."   Acad. 36:
   421.

(Fyfe, H. H.)   "Charley's Aunt" on the Continent.   The. n. s.
   25: 338 (Je. '95).
   Pinero's Plays as Literature.   The. n. s. 26: 323 (D. '95).
   Mr. Grundy as Cassandra.   The. n. s. 27: 203 (Ap.'96).

Gag.   B. H. Dixon.   The. '81, 2: 208.

(Galdemar, A.)   Sardou's "Thermidor."   Fortn. 57: 770
   (Je. '92).

Gallery. Gods and Galleries. Tinsley 10: 592.
Among the Gods. (M. Pemberton) The. n. s. 20: 74
(Ag. '92).
Gallery Scenes, Irish. Harper 42: 505 (F. '71).
Pit and Gallery Wit. The. n. s. 16: 117 (Ag. '90).
The Maligned Gods. The. n. s. 24: 8 (Jl.'94).

Gallery, Footmen's. (D. Cook) Once a Week 15: 594.

Gannon, Mary. (L. C. Davis) Galaxy 6: 245.

(Gardnice, J.). Historic Element in Sir John Falstaff. Fortn.
19: 333.

(Garland, Hamlin.) American Drama. Lit. World (Bost.)
20: 304.

Garrick, David. Harper 69: 53. (H. W. Alden) Harper
37: 172 (Jl. '68). (J. Winsor) Atlan. 22: 79 (Jl.'68).
All the Year 19: 346. Belgra. 5: 99. Chamb. J. 45:
294. (R. B. Knowles) Dub. Univ. 95: 207. Quart.
125: 1. Same art. Liv. Age 98: 451. Temp. Bar 52:
70. Same art. Ecl. M. 90: 336. Dub. Univ. 70: 339.
Same art. Liv. Age 96: 309. (P. Fitzgerald) Gent. M.
n. s. 18: 561.
Acting of, as Seen in his own Time. (W. H. Pollock)
Longm. 6: 37.
and Acting. Anal. M. 5: 65.
as Actor and Manager. Temp. Bar 11: 336.
and his Fellow Actors. (J. F. Molloy) Eng. Illust. 5:
189.
First Appearance of. (P. Fitzgerald) Theatre '86, 1:
308.
Last Appearance of. (A. Dobson) Longm. 26: 590
(O. '95).
and Geo. Coleman. "Clandestine Marriage." (P. H.
Fitzgerald) The. n. s. 9: 340.
and his Contemporaries. Colburn. 32: 273.
Correspondence of. Mod. R. 126: 167; 127: 321.
Delivery of a Passage of Shakspere. Colburn 4: 551.

Garrick, David. Farewell to the Stage. All the Year 18: 87.
 as Hamlet. (Lord B. Lytton) Fortn. 15: 221. Same
  art. Liv. Age 09, 67, 236.
 and Dr. Johnson. No. Am. 4: 38.
 Letters of. Lon. M. 2: 647; 3: 202. Colburn 34: 196.
 Life of. (P. Fitzgerald) Dub. Univ. 65: 243, 396, 603;
  66: 553; 67: 85, 274, 384; 68: 434, 560, 678; 69: 65,
  212, 573; 70: 84, 213, 339. So. R. n. s. 7: 31.
 Knight's Life of. Ath. 2: 329 (S. 8,'94).
 and Murphy, Quarrel of. (T. F. Ordish) Bibliog. 6: 37,
  65.
 New Facts Regarding. Colburn 34: 568.
 Recollections of. Westm. 17: 67. Blackw. 18: 488. Mus.
  8: 78.
 Rivals and Associates of. Temp. Bar 54: 86.
 and Shakspere Jubilee. (D. Cook) Once a Week. 10:
  104.
 and the Shakspere Revival. Temp. Bar 86: 496.
 and Mrs. Siddons, Theatrical Farewells of. Ev. Sat. 4:
  161.
 and his Wife. Ecl. M. 45: 139. Harper 51: 792 (N.
  '72).

Garrick Club, at the. Spec. 55: 1613.
 Theatrical Portraits. (J. W. (Cole,) Calcraft) Dub. Univ.
  42: 643; 43: 223, 393.

(Garrison, W.) Edw. Fitzgerald's Letters to F. Kemble.
 Nation 61: 297 (O. '24, '95).

Gerard, Florence. The. '80, 2: 319.

German Drama. (J. Pollock) Contemp. 21: 335. Colburn
 4: 145.
 Modern. (E. Brain) The. n. s. 25: 84 (F. '95).
 and French Drama. (J. Pollock) Contemp. 21: 335.
 and Early English (W. J. Thones) Colburn 61: 19. (S.
  Whitman) Chaut. 21: 163 (My. '95).
 and Its Authors. (F. Spielhagen) Cosmop. 17: 177
  (Je. '94).

German Drama. Court Theatre, Twenty-five Years of a. (J. G. Robertson) National 25: 247 (Ap. '95).
    Theatres. (C. Hervey) The. '85, 2: 140.
    Plays and Actors. For. Quar. R. 32: 197.
    Literature of Tragedy. Blackw. 18: 286.
    Berlin Theatre, Hundred Years of. Ecl. M. 63: 187.

German Dramatic Literature. (C. S. Hartmann) Amer. 12: 39.

German Playwrights. (T. Carlyle) For. Quar. R. 3: 94.

German Stage. (S. Baxter) Atlan. 42: 177. (D. E. Bandemann) Macmil. 33: 430.
    Glance at. (H. S. Wilson) Gent. M. n. s. 14: 687.

German Theatre. (A. Stutzer) Belgra. 28: 476.

German Tragedy, Modern. (R. P. Gillies) For. Quar. R. 1: 565.

Gesticulation. Tinsley 10: 656.
    Italian. Dub. R. 3: 1.
    Philosophy of Gesture. Portf. 10: 621; 11: 38.

Ghosts on the Stage. Temp. Bar 8: 503. (W. J. Lawrence) Gent. M. n. s. 39: 545. Same art. Ecl. M. 110: 210.

Gilbert, John. Harper 79: 634 (S. '89). (J. R. Towse) Cent. 13: 378. Critic 14: 309.
    in "She Stoops to Conquer." Harper 73: 308 (Jl. '86).

(Gilbert, John.) Moral Influence of the Stage. No. Am. 136: 581.

Gilbert, Mrs. The. '86, 2: 106.

Gilbert, Wm. Schwenk. The. '83, 1: 217. (Kate Field) Scribner 18: 751 (S. '79). (A. Winton) The. n. s. 14: 71. Lond. Soc. 27: 13. (K. Field) Scrib. 18: 751. (W. D. Adams) Belgra. 45: 438. (W. Archer) St. James 49: 287. Dark Blue 4: 707. Once a Week 28: 117. (W. D. Adams) The. n. s. 24: 286 (D. '94).
    At Home. Critic 19: 310.
    Brantingame Hall. The. n. s. 13: 62.
    Humors of. (P. Fitzgerald) The. '81, 2: 339.

Gilbert, Wm. Schwenk. The Spirit of His Comedies. (A. F. Marshall) Month 55 : 254.

and Sir A. Sullivan. Operettas. Harper 72 : 476 (F. '86). The. n. s. 15 : 59.

"Iolanthe." The. '83, 1 : 20. Sat. R. 54 : 764 (?).

"Mikado" (W. B. Kingston) The. '85, 1 : 186. Sat. R. 59 : 378.

"Mountebanks." Gent. M. n. s. 48 : 206 (F. '92). The. n. s. 19 : 112 (F. '92).

"Patience." The. '81, 1 : 352.

"Pirates of Penzance." (W. B. Kingston) The. '85, 1 : 80.

"Princess Ida." (W. B. Kingston) The. '84, 1 : 75. Sat. R. 57 : 49.

"Ruddygore." (F. Wedmore) Acad. 31 : 118. Sat. R. 63 : 157. The. n. s. 9 : 95.

Gilchrist, Connie. The. '81, 1 : 41.

Gilchrist's True Story of Hamlet. (G. E. Woodberry) Nation 48 : 273.

(Giles, H.) Influence of Shakspere. Chr. Exam. 67 : 178.

(Gildersleeve, B. L.) Æschylus's "Agamemnon" at Oxford, 1880. Nation 30 : 472.

Gillette, Wm. "Held by the Enemy." The. n. s. 9 : 281.

(Gillette, Wm.) Will Drama Live? Dr. Mirror, 23 : 578 (Jan. 25, '90).

(Gillfillan, G.) Hamlet. Ecl. M. 24 : 61.

(Gillies, R. P.) Modern German Tragedy. For. Quar. R. 1 : 565.

Gilman, Caroline Howard. (J. P. R. Dorr) Critic 13 : 151.

Girardin on the Drama. For. Quar. R. 33 : 33. Same art. Ecl. M. 3 : 33.

(Goddard, H. P.) Recollections of E. L. Davenport. Lippinc. 21 : 463.

Lesson of "Cymbeline." Poet Lore 3 : 572.

(**Grubb**, S. F.) Falstaff. Western 6 : 370.

Grundy, Sydney. "A Fool's Paradise." (M. de Meusiaux)
The. n. s. 13 : 157.
"The Snowball." (M. de Meusiaux) The. n. s. 9 : 274.
"A Pair of Spectacles." Sat. R. 69 : 260.
"A Village Priest." Sat. R. 69 : 436.
and the Critics. (M. Watson) The. n. s. 24 : 161 (O.'94).
as Cassandra. (H. H. Fyfe) The. n. s. 27 : 203 (Ap.'96).

(**Grundy**, Sydney,) Marching to Our Doom. The. n. s. 27 :
131, 196 (Mr. & Ap.'96)
Dramatic Construction. The. '81, 1 : 208.
Dramatic Ring. The, '79, 2 : 273.
Dearth of Originality. The. 2 : 274.

(**Gruneisen**, G. L.) Lyric Drama. St. James 36 : 363.

(**Guthrie**, F. A.) Humors of a Minor Theatre. Harper 76 :
727 (Ap.'88).
London Music Halls. Harper 82 : 190 (Ja.'91).

Gwynn, Nell. (D. Cook) Gent. M. n. s. 30 : 489. (J. F.
Molloy) Eng. Illust. 3 : 541. Same art. Ecl. M. 107 :
263. (P. Cunningham) Gent. M. n. s. 35 : 30, 115,
253, 339, 501, 609 ; 36 : 33, 136. (Ja. to Ag.'51.)
(Mrs. S. C. Hall) Internat. 3 : 9. The. n. s. 22 : 282.
As an Actress. Temp. Bar 53 : 559.
Letters of. Blackw. 3 : 547.
and Sayings of Charles II. Liv. Age 34 : 397.
and Lord Rochester's Poems. Ecl. M. 26 : 512. Liv. Age
34 : 28.

(**Gwynn**, S. L.) Songs of Shakspere. Acad. 48 : 369 (N.'95).
Recollections of. Colburn 54 : 87.

Gwynne, Julia. The. '84, 2 : 1, 42.

("**H. H.**") *See " Helen Hunt Jackson."*

Hackett, James H. Galaxy 14 : 550 (O.'72).
Falstaff of. Harper 35 : 394 (Ag.'67).

Hading, Jane. (H. St. Maur) Munsey 14: 159 (N.'95). Coquelin and. Critic 13: 193, 207.

(Hading, Jane.) Story of my Career. Cosmop. 6: 220.

(Hales, J. W.) Shakspere and the Jews. Eng. Hist. R. 9: 652 (O. '94).

(Hale, E. E., Jr.) Renascence of the Drama. Dial (Ch.) 21: 149 (S. 16, '96).

(Hale, W. S.) Joseph Jefferson's Birthplace. Dr. Mirror, 35: 886 (Xmas '95).

Halévy, L. (J. B. Matthews) Lippinc. 26: 711.

(Halie, E.) Beauty on the French Stage. Cosmop. 10: 515.

(Hall, F. M. Howe.) Edwin Booth and Julia Ward Howe. N. Eng. M. n. s. 9: 315 (N.'93).

(Hall, G. S.) The Passion Play in 1880. Nation 31: 110.

(Hall, Mrs. S. C.) Nell Gwynn. Internat. M. 3: 9.

(Hall, N., and H. C. Shuttleworth.) Duty of the Church as to the Theatre. Ch. Lit. 11: 302 (S. '94).

(Hallam, A.) "Coriolanus" on the Stage. The. '79, 2: 22.

(Hamer, J.) Shakspere. Belgra. 78: 398 (Ag.'92). Women of Shakspere. Belgra. 77: 304 (Mr.'92).

Hamilton, Henry, and Mark Quinton. (C. Howard) The. n. s. 17: 310.

Hamlet. (D. Dorchester) Meth. R. 52: 390 (My.'92). (W. Barrett) Lippinc. 45: 580. (J. E. Murdoch) Forum 9: 496 (Je. '90). (A. Oehlenschlager) Scand. 1: 234. (J. R. Lowell) No. Am. 106: 629. Blackw. 2: 504; 24: 585; 37: 236. Fraser 14: 1. So. R. 3: 380. (G. Gillfillan) Ecl. M. 24: 61. Anal. M. 5: 68. New Eng. M. 5: 458. (H. N. Hudson) Am. Whig R. 7: 94, 121. (E. F. Mosby) So. M. 9: 348. (R. G. White) Galaxy 9: 535. (C. H. Bull, Jr.) Poet Lore 3: 615. (Appleton Morgan) Cath. World 44: 29.

Age of. (M. Thomas) Ath. '84, 2: 703.

and Antonio's Revenge. (L. M. Griffiths) Poet Lore 2: 414.

Hamlet and Ophelia. (Carolyn Evans Huse) Looker On 3 :
417 (N.'96). (H. Irving) 19th Cent. 1 : 513.

Belleforest's. House. Words 16 : 545.

F. R. Benson as. The. 24 : 212. Sat. R. 69 : 315.

Booth as. *See " Booth."*

a Century of. (L. Hutton) Harper 79 : 866 (N.'89).

and Don Quixote. (I. Tourgénieff) Fortn. 62 : 191.

A Fat Man. (C. Edwards) Contin. M. 1 : 571 (My. '62).

Fechter as. *See " Fechter."*

From an Actor's Prompt Book. (Herbert Beerbohm
Tree) Fortn. Dec. '95.

Ghost of. Fraser 32 : 350.

Gilchrist's True Story of. (G. E. Woodberry) Nation
48 : 273.

Irving as. *See " Irving."*

Insanity of. (W. Farrar) Lon. M. 9 : 373, 647. Victoria 10 : 204.

Life and Philosophy of. Sharpe 19 : 233.

Lawrence and Kemble's (M. C. Clarke) Sharp. 6 : 181.

Loneliness of. (E. Ferrier) Evang. R. 21 : 210.

Madness of, Feigned. Blackw. 46 : 449. (L. Blanchard)
Colburn 68 : 93. (H. B. Lathrop) Acad. (Syr.) 7 :
89 (Mr. '92). (R. C. MacDonald) Acad. (Syr.) 7 :
29 (F. '92).

Maiming of. (A. C. Botkin) Lakeside 9 : 444.

Myths of. (E. Schuyler) Nation 10 : 170.

A Northern. (E. Rose) Fraser 95 : 609.

How Old Was He ? All the Year 39 : 104.

Saga of. (C. De Falbe) 19th Cent. 12 : 947.

Sanity of. Foster's Mo. Ref. 1 : 11.

and the Playwrights. All the Year 34 : 5.

Psychological Study of. (A. A. Lipscomb) Meth. Q. 44 :
665.

Rossi as. *" See Rossi."*

Something touching Lord (A. Morgan) Cath. World 44 :
29.

Study of. (H. C. Pedder) Manhat. 1 : 321.

Hamlet, Subjection of. (C. S. Patterson) Amer. 5 : 185.
> of the Seine. (Lady Pollock) 19th Cent. 20 : 805 (D. '86).
> Tree as. *See " Tree."*
> " Poor Yorick." (E. A. Wood) The. n. s. 16 : 213 ; 26 : 77.
> Where he Came From. (C. De Falbe) 1 : 132.
> Whiteside as. *See " Walker Whiteside."*
> Wilson Barrett as. *See " W. Barrett."*
> Voltairean. St. Paul's 9 : 173. Same art. Liv. Age
> 111 : 791.

" Hamlet." (G. Dawson) Peop. J. 7 : 279. (D. Cook) Once a
> Week 11 : 621. (D. J. Snider) J. Spec. Philos. 7 : (Ap.)
> 67, (July) 78. (W. H. Browne) So. M. 15 : 106. So.
> R. n. s. 7 : 271 ; 8 : 116 ; 24 : 426. All the Year 42 : 138,
> 173. Blackw. 37 : 236. Same art Mus. 26 : 545. Dub.
> Univ. 88 : 88. (E. Falconer) The. '79, 1 : 171. (C. Scott)
> The. '84, 2 : 243. (F. Leifchild) Contemp. 43 : 31.
> A difficulty in (J. P. Quincy) Atlan. 49 : 388.
> Allegory in. (W. W. Crane) Poet Lore 3 : 565.
> Analyzed, Westm. 83 : 65.
> Byron and Shelley on. Colburn 29 : 327.
> at the Comédie Française. (C. Seymour) Poet Lore
> 1 : 571 (D. '89).
> and the Critics (E. Roscoe) Victoria 20 : 502.
> of the Day. (Lady Hardy) The. 79 : 1, 17.
> Difficulty about. Fraser 99 : 394.
> Gervinus's Criticism on (E. Roscoe) Victoria 21 : 338.
> Ghost in. (F. C. Burnand) Month 64 : 64. (G. Mc-
> Donald) Macmil. 34 : 351.
> Goethe on. (H. S. Wilson) Lond. Soc. 28 : 308.
> a Greek. Fraser 102 : 511.
> The Last. Colburn 152 : 279.
> Macdonald's Study of. Sat. R. 39 : 243.
> and " Macbeth " at the Lyceum (M. Seton) Colburn 168 :
> 178.
> and the Modern Stage. (M. Morris) Macmil. 65 : 357
> (Mr. '92).

(**Harris**, M. C.) Playwright's Novitiate. Atlan. 74: 515
(Ag. '94).

Harris, Sir Augustus. The. '81, 1: 322, 341. The. n. s.
27: 5 (Jl. '96).

(**Harris**, Sir A.) Drury Lane Theatre. Fortn. 45: 603.

(**Harrison**, Fred'k.) Revival of the Drama. Forum 16: 184
(O. '93).

(**Hart**, J. M.) German Criticism of Shakspere. Putnam 16:
353, 562.

(**Hart**, K.) Oaths in Shakspere. Poet Lore 3: 113.

(**Hart**, E. J.) Romeos Ancient and Modern. The. '82, 1:
148.

(**Hartman**, C. S.) Dramatic Literature in Germany. Amer.
12: 39.

Harvey, James Clarence. "The Players." Munsey 12: 581
(Mr.'95).

(**Hatton**, Joseph.) "Becket" at the Lyceum. Art. J. 45:
105 (Ap.'93).
"Faust" on the English Stage. Art. J. 38: 57, 88.
Henry Irving at Home. Harper 64: 382 (F.'82).
H. J. Montague and America. The. '78, 2: 208.
Irving in Holland and Belgium. Art. J. 38: 207, 245.

(**Hausknecht**, Emil.) Shakspere in Japan. Poet Lore 1: 466
(O. '89).

(**Haweis**, H. R.) Oratorio and the Drama. Harper 70: 109
(D. '89).

(**Haweis**, M. E.) The Ballet. St. Paul 12: 324.

(**Hawkins**, Fred'k.) Social Position of the Actor in France.
The. n. s. 26: 6 (Je.'95).
"Becket." The. 1: 53.
Hippolyte Clarion. The. '86, 1: 291; 2: 20.
Foyer of the Comédie Française. The. '79, 1: 360.
Origin of the Comédie Française. The. '79, 1: 286.

Henley, W. E., Plays of.   Gent. M. n. s. 49 : 529 (N.'92).
  and Robt. L. Stevenson. "Macaire." Sat. R. 79 : 756
    (N. '95).
  Tommaso Salvini. National 3 : 199 (Ap. '84). Same art.
    Liv. Age 164 : 468.
  Coöperation of Actors. The. '80, 2 : 274.

(Hennequin, Alfred.)   Characteristic of American Drama.
    Arena 1 : 700.
  Drama of the Future. Arena 3 : 385.
  The Good Old Ways. Dr. Mirror 23 : 592. (M. 3,'90).
  Writing for the Stage. Forum 8 : 705 (F.'96).

Henri, Blanche.   The. '79, 2 : 94.

"Henry IV." Part I. All the Year 53 : 30. Part II. All
    the Year 53 : 53.

(Herand, J. A.)   Macbeth. Peop. J. 8 : 69, 78, 89.

(Herford, C. H.)   Henrik Ibsen. Acad. 41 : 247 (Mr. 12,
    '92).
  Henrik Ibsen's Earlier Work. Lippinc. 49 : 351 (Mr.
    '92).
  Recent German Works on Shakspere. Acad. 46 : 44 (Jl.
    21, '94).

(Herford, C. S. A.)   Two Thousand Years of Comedy. N.
    Eng. M. 53 : 441.

Herman, Henry, and F. Wells. "Golden Band." (C. Howard)
    The. 19 : 49.

Her Majesty's Theatre.   (W. D'Arcy) Belgra. 4 : 416.

Hermione, Shakspere's Character of. (Lady Martin)
    Blackw. 149 : 1.
  The Cutting-out of. (F. H. Pellew) Gent. M. n. s.
    47 : 519.

Hermiones, Some Famous. (C. E. L. Wingate) Cosmop.
    10 : 314.

(Hersee, H.)   Opera Bouffe. The. '78, 2 : 281.

(**Hervey,** C.) French Actors and Actresses. Colburn 83: 577.
Gossip about Actors. The. 84, 2: 174.
Actors, How they Fared in French Revolution. Longm.
7: 309.
Comédie Française. The. '84, 2: 1.
Drama in Paris. Colburn 81: 484.
Drama in Paris since Revolution. Colburn 83: 255, 388.
Theatres in Florence. The. '85, 2: 35.
Foyers of Paris Theatres. *See " Foyers."*
German Theatres. The. '85, 2: 140.
An Habitue's Note-Book. *See " Drama."*

(**Hervey,** R. K.) A Word to Actors. The. n. s. 10: 133.

(**Hetherington,** J. N.) Fools of Shakspere. Cornh. 40:
722.

(**Hexamer,** C. J.) Construction of Theatre. J. Frank. Inst.
134: 43 (Je. '92).

(**Heywood,** Thos.) A Woman Killed with Kindness. Acad.
34: 375. (F. Marshall) The. 18: 205.

(**Heywood,** Thos., 2nd.) Uses and Abuses of Burlesque.
Tinsley 37: 477.

Hicks, Mr. Seymour, Portrait of, in " Under the Clock."
The. 23: 146 (Mr. '94).

(**Hill,** Barton.) Personal Recollections of Edwin Booth. Dr.
Mirror 37: 939. (Xmas, '96).

(**Hill,** F. H.) Irving's " Henry VIII." Contemp. 61: 73 (Ja.
'92).

Hill, J. W., in " Private Secretary." The. '85, 1: 69.

Hillhouse, J. A., Dramas and Discourses of. Chr. Exam. 27:
285. (J. G. Palfrey) No. Am. 50: 231.

(**Hilliard,** Kate.) V. Hugo, Dramatist, Novelist, and Poet.
Lippinc. 9: 188 (F. '72).

(**Hillman,** S. D.) Modern Theatre and the Attic Tragedy.
Met. 18: 341.

Hilton, Hilda. The. '81, 2: 125.

Hindu Drama. Ed. R. 108: 253. (E. Everett) No. Am. 26: 111. Blackw. 34: 715; 35: 122. Westm. 54: 1. Ed. R. 22: 400. Quart. 45: 39. (Mrs. Postans) Sharpe 11: 212.
> History and Character of. Westm. 67: 364.

Hindu Theatre, Wilson on. Ed. R. 48: 328.

Hiss and its History. Lippinc. 22: 781 (D. '78).
> Natural History of, in Theatres. (L. Robinson) No. Am. 157: 104 (Jl.'93).
> The Right to. The. '83, 2: 178.

Hissing at the Theatres. Harper 70: 487.
> in Theatres. All the Year 28: 468.
> in Theatres. (W. H. Pollock) The. n. s. 147 (Mr.'95).

Historical Drama and the Teaching of History. (H. E. Edgarton) National 17: 743.

Histrionics, The Grand Old Days of. (O. Logan) Harper 69: 48 (Je.'79).

History of the Stage, Fleay's. Poet Lore 3: 149 (Mr.'91.).

Hobsen, Maud, Portrait of. The. n. s. 24: 12 (Jl.'94.)

(Hodell, C. W.) The Opening Scenes in Shakspere's Plays. Poet Lore. 6: 169, 337, 452 (Ap., Je., Ag. '94).

(Hogan, J. F.) Australian Theatre. The. n. s. 14: 296 (D. '89).

(Hogarth, G.) The Claque System. Bentley 4: 591.

Holcroft, Thos. English Dom. M. 16: 133. Temp. Bar 54: 469.

(Holland, E. G.) "King Richard III." Contin. Mo. 2: 320.

Hollingshead, John. (J. Knight) The. n. s. 26: 26 (Jl. '85).
> Shakspere and. (W. C. Pell) Harper 23: 486 (S.'61).

(Hollingshead, J.) Kate Vaughan. The. n. s. 27: 257 (My.'96).

(**Hollingshead**, J.) Salaries of Actors. The. '79, 1 : 107.

Theatrical Bricks and Mortar. The. n. s. 28 : 73 (Ag.
'96).

(**Holme**, G.) The Story of Faust. Munsey 10: 401 (Jan.
'94).

Honolulu, Drama in. (C. W. Stoddard) Overland n. s. 2 : 118.

(**Hooker**, I. B.) Anna Dickinson. Nation 7: 391.

(**Hooper**, Lucy H.) Alex. Dumas, *fils*. Lippinc. 21 : 501
(Ap. '78).

Paris Theatres. Appleton 11 : 525, 583, 626; 12 : 454, 716.

The Teacher of Rachel. Lippinc. 29 : 617 (Je. '82).

(**Hope**, Anthony, and Edw. Rose.) "Prisoner of Zenda."
(L. B. Ellis) Illust. (Je. and Jl. '96).

Hopeful View, A. (Edw. A. Dithmar) Dr. Mirror 23 : 591.
(Ap. 26, '90).

(**Hopkins**, F.) Plays, Players, and Playwrights. Dub. Univ.
93 : 210.

Hopper, Chas. II. "Chimmie Fadden." (B. Fletcher)
Godey 132 : 361 (Ap. '96).

(**Hornblow**, Arthur.) French Contemporary Dramatists.
Cosmop. 15 : 107 (My. '93).

American Dramatists. Munsey 12: 159 (D. '94).

Children on the Stage. Munsey 12: 32 (O. '94).

Favorites of the Paris Stage. Munsey 11 : 479, 591 (Ag.
S. '94).

Some Paris Stage Beauties. Godey 127: 65 (Jl. '93).

(**Horne**, R. H.) Bygone Celebrities. Gent. M. n. s. 6: 247,
660; 7 : 88, 468.

Hosken, Jas. Dryden. (E. D. A. Morehead) Acad. 42 : 125
(Ag. 13, '92). Spec. 69 : 230 (Ag. 13, '92).

(**Hosmer**, J. K.) College Theatricals. Atlan. 30 : 19 (Jl.
'72). Nation 10 : 6.

(**Houghton**, Philip.) Duse as Camille. The. n. s. 23 : 303
(Je. '94).

Houssaye, M. Arsène. (R. Davey) The. n. s. 27: 271 (My. '96).

(House, E. H.) A Day in a Japanese Theatre. Atlan. 30: 257.

(Hovey, Rich'd.) Maurice Maeterlinck. 19th Cent. 37: 491 (Mr.'95).

(Howard, Arthur Weyburn.) V. Sardou. Munsey 12: 137 (D.'94).

Howard, Bronson. "Henrietta." The. n. s. 7: 250.
   "Truth." The. n. s. 16: 190.
   The Plays of. Cent. 3: 465.

(Howard, Bronson) Old Dry Ink. Dr. Mirror 37: 939 (Xmas, '96).

(Howard, Cecil.) The Bancrofts. The. 20: 250; 21: 57.
   R. W. Buchanan and F. Herman's "Blue Bells of Scotland." The. n. s. 10: 219.
   Difficulties of Criticism. The. n. s. 25: 218 (Ap.'95).
   Daly's Company in "As You Like It." The. n. s. 16: 90.
   Herman and Wills, "The Golden Band." The. n. s. 10: 49.
   "Joseph's Sweetheart." The. n. s. 11: 212.
   Mrs. Langtry in "Antony and Cleopatra." The. n. s. 16: 287.
   Henry Neville as Jack Holt. The. n. s. 19: 155 (Mr. '92).

Howe, Henry, Reminiscences of. (J. Coleman; Geo. W. Bayham) The. n. s. 27: 263 (Mr.'96).

(Howe, M. A. De W.) Stratford Jubilee, 1769. Harv. Mo. 6: 96.

Howe, Julia Ward, Edwin Booth and. (F. M. H. Hall) N. Eng. M. 9: 315 (N.'93).

(Howe, Julia Ward.) "Hamlet" at the Boston. Atlan. 3: 172.

(Howells, Wm. Dean.) A New Taste in Theatricals (Burlesques). Atlan. 23: 635.
   John T. Raymond as Colonel Sellers. Atlan. 35: 749.

(Howitt, M.) Charlotte Cushman. Peop. J. 2: 30, 47.

(Hubert, P. G.) New York's Lyceum School for Actors. Lippinc. 35: 483 (My.'85).

(Hudson, W. H.) Introducing American Audiences on English Stage. The. n. s. 10: 255.
English Drama during Commonwealth. The. n. s. 10: 177.
English Religious Drama and its Stage Arrangements. Antiq. n. s. 15: 62.
At the Old Globe Theatre. The. n. s. 15: 173.

(Hudson, H. N.) Character of Macbeth. Am. Whig R. 6: 581.
Hamlet. Am. Whig R. 7: 94, 121.

(Hughes, Thos. P.) The Stage from a Clergyman's Point of View. Forum 20: 695 (F.'96).

Hugo, Victor. (K. Hilliard) Lippinc. 9: 188 (F. '72). (J. B. Matthews) Scrib. 22: 688. (C. Barrère) Macmil. 30: 281. (F. Kemble) No. Am. 43: 133. Am. Q. 19: 167. Westm. 34: 287. Select J. 3: 57. For. Quar. R. 6: 455; 8: 196; 17: 193. Dem. R. 13: 378.
and Shakspere. Amer. 14: 7.
"Hernani." Am. Mo. M. 9: 41.
"Hernani." First Performance of. Ev. Sat. 11: 151.

Humors of a Minor Theatre (F. A. Guthrie) Harper 76: 727 (Ap.'88).

Humor, New, and Non-Humorists. (J. L. Toole.) National 21: 449 (Je.'93).

(Humphrey, G. E.) Mary Anderson as Juliet. National 4: 812 (F.'85).

(Hunt, H. M.) Miracle Play of 1870 at Bethlehem, N. H. Atlan. 20: 732.

(**Hunt,** W. S.)   Early Work of Henry Irving.   The. n. s. 23:
198 (Ap. '94).

(**Hunting,** G. D.)   Moral Purpose in the Modern Drama.
The. n. s. 19: 121 (Mr. '92).

(**Huse,** Carolyn Evans.)   Hamlet and Ophelia.   Looker-On 3:
417 (N. '96).

Hutton Laurence.   Curiosities of American Stage.   Harper
82: 63 (Mr. '91).

Hutton, Laurence, and J. B. Matthews' "American Actors and
Actresses."   Atlan. 39: 421.   Cent. 2: 468.

(**Hutton,** Laurence.)   American Drama.   Lippinc. 37: 289.
American Burlesque, The.   Harper 81: 59.
Century of Hamlest, A.   Harper 79: 866 (N. '89).
Comedy, A Half-forgotten.   Dr. Mirror 23: 584 (My.
8, '90).
Infant Phenomena.   Les. Mo. 21: 4 (Ap. '86).
Negro on the Stage, The.   Harper 79: 131 (Je. '89).
"Look here upon this Picture."   Harper 82: 488.

Iago.   Cornh. 33: 91.   *See also " Othello."*

Iago's Conscience.   (A. M. Spence) Poet Lore 5: 194 (Ap.
'93).

Ibsen, Henrik.   Harper 78: 984 (My. '89).   (R. B. Anderson) Amer. 4: 8.   (H. H. Boyesen) Cent. 16: 794 (Mr.
'90).   (G. R. Carpenter) Scrib. 5: 404 (Ap. '89).   (C.
H. Herford) Acad. 41: 247 (Mr. 12, '92).   (A. N.
Meyer) Lippinc. 53: 375 (Mr. '94).   (F. Sarcey)
Cosmop. (Je. '96).   (A. Schovelin) Scand. 1: 11, 113.
(W. L. Courtney) Fortn. 63: 277 (F. '95).
and the Morbid Taint.   Belgra. 83: 59 (Ja. '94).
and the Students of Christiania.   Scand. 2: 311.
as an Artist.   (L. Simons) Westm. 140: 506 (N.
'93).
at Christiania.   (E. J. Goodman) The. n. s. 26: 146 (S.
'95).

(**Inglis**, F.) Italian Drama. No. Am. 39 : 329.

"**Ingomar**," Mary Anderson in. The. '83, 2 : 199.

Innocuous, A Plea for the. (R. C. Carton) The. n. s. 25 : 154 (Mr. '95).

Inspiration and Naturalism in Acting. (H. Irving) Educa. 5 : 591. *See also " Emotionalism."*

(**Ireland**, F. G.) "Phormio" at Harvard. Educa. R. 8 : 54 (Je. '94).

Irish Actors of the 18th Century. Dub. Univ. 62 : 3.
 Drama. Old Dublin Stage. (H. B. Baker) Belgra. 39 : 304.
 Dramatists. (J. W. (Cole) Calcraft) Dub. Univ. 45 : 39, 527; 46 : 38, 548; 47 : 15, 359.
 Gallery Scenes. Harper 42 : 505 (F. '71).
 Theatre Royal, Dublin. (J. W. (Cole) Calcraft) Dub. Univ. 72 : 454, 558.
 Theatricals. Dub. Univ. 35 : 117, 362.

Irving, Sir Henry. Harper 64 : 382; 68 : 314; 69 : 308; 71 : 148 (Je. '85). Sat. R. 55 : 731; 56 : 13, 148. The. '78, 2 : 43; '84, 1 : 32; '81, 1 : 151. The. n. s. 25 : 129 (Mr. '95); 26 : 1 (Jl. '95). (H. A. Clapp) Atlan. 53 : 413. (R. L. Collier) Lippinc. 32 : 441 (N. '83). (J. Leyland) Amer. 6 : 312; 7 : 122, 141. (F. Hawkins) Dial (Ch.) 4 : 277. (J. R. Towse) Cent. 5 : 660 (Mr. '84). (W. Winter) The. '84, 2 : 43, 86. (L. F. Austin) Victoria 22 : 169. (A. Lewis) Dub. Univ. 90 : 284. Victoria 28 : 441. Temp. Bar 38 : 393; 39 : 547.
 as Actor and Artist. (L. J. Claris) The. '82, 1 : 155.
 in America. Sat. R. 56 : 693; 57 : 606, 795.
 at Home. (J. Hatton) Harper 64 : 382 (F. '82).
 as a Tragedian. (B. Brooksbank) National 1 : 16.
 and English Drama. (G. Barlow) New R. 7 : 665 (D.'92).
 and Diderot's "Paradoxe." (J. Ramsay) National 3 : 99 (Mr. '84). *See " Emotionalism."*
 and Salvini. Gent. M. n. s. 14 : 609.

Irving, Sir Henry, and the Dignity of the Stage. Sat. R. 79:
182 (F. 9, '95).
   and Miss Terry. Harper 69: 303 (Ag. '84).
   and his Work. (A. S. Fitch) Manhat. 2: 391. (E. R.
Russell) Fortn. 22: 401.
   as Becket. (H. D. Traill) Acad. 44: 197 (S. 2, '93).
   as Hamlet. The. '80, 2: 354. Temp. Bar 55: 398.
Macmil. 31: 236. Belgra. 25: 182. All the Year 33:
179. Victoria 24: 169. The. '79, 1: 339.
   as King Arthur. (J. W. Cunliffe) Canad. M. 6: 75
(N. '95).
   as King Lear. (E. R. Russell) 19th Cent. 33: 44
(Ja. '93). (H. J. Jennings) Gent. M. n. s. 49: 624,
634 (D. '92). Sat. R. 74: 676 (D. 10, '92). The. n.
s. 20: 278 (D. '92).
   as Macbeth. (A. G. L.) Poet Lore 1: 46 (Ja. '89).
   as Shylock. Appleton 23: 84.
   as Wolsey. The. n. s. 19: 101 (F. '92).
   Coquelin and. (D. Boucicault) No. Am. 145: 158.
   A French View of. (J. Claretie) The. '79, 2: 16.
   Harvard College, Address at. Critic 24: 204 (Mr. 24, '94).
   How, Rose to Fame. (H. St. Maur) Munsey 14: 652
(Mr. '96).
   in "The Bells." (J. R. Towse) Nation 37: 369. Once a
Week 26: 57.
   in "Faust." Spec. 58: 1753. Sat. R. 61: 48; 62: 89.
(W. L. Courtney) Fortn. 45: 102. (W. H. Pollock)
Lippinc. 27: 443 (Ap. '86).
   in Henry VIII. (F. H. Hill) Contemp. 61: 73 (Ja.
'92). Gent. M. n. s. 48: 209 (F. '92).
   in "Merchant of Venice." Harper 68: 314 (F. '84). The.
'80, 1: 16.
   in "Much Ado." Sat. R. 54: 536. Spec. 55: 1312.
(F. Hawkins) The. '82, 2: 212, 294.
   in "Romeo and Juliet." Sat. R. 53: 299. The. '82,
1: 233. Spec. 55: 325. (F. Wedmore) Acad. 21: 200.
   in "Twelfth Night." (J. Knight) The. '84, 2: 55.

Irving, Sir Henry, in "Waterloo." (A. Brereton) The. n. s.
24: 179 (O. '94).

in Holland and Belgium. (J. Hatton) Art J. 38: 207, 245.

in the Provinces. The. '78, 2: 169. The. '83, 2: 196.

in the Ridiculous. Sat. R. 79: 619 (My. '95).

in Shaksperian Characters. (E. R. Russell) Fortn.
40: 466. (F. Wedmore) Acad. 22: 303.

Influence of. (W. T. W. Ball) New Eng. M. n. s. 10:
173 (Ap. '94).

Influence in America, The. (Stephen Fiske) Dr. Mirror.
See " Fiske."

The Knighting of. Sat. R. 79: 718 (Ja. 1, '95).

Ladies' Debate on. The. '83, 1: 78, 193.

on the Art of Acting. (L. de la Ramée) ("Ouida")
19th Cent. 37: 786 (My. '95). *See " Emotionalism."*

on the English Drama. (E. A. Barron) Dial (Ch.)
15: 90.

on a Municipal Theatre. The. n. s. 24: 211 (N. '94).

on the Position of the Actor. The. n. s. 25: 125 (Mr. '95).

Second Tour. The. '84, 2: 227; '85, 1: 27, 237.

Stage Management of. (W. H. Pollock) Cent. 4: 953
(O. '83).

(Irving, Sir Henry.) Actor Management. 19th Cent. 26:
1040 (Je. '90).

An Actor's Notes of Shakspere. I. Third Murderer in
"Macbeth." II. Hamlet and Ophelia. III. "Look here
upon this picture, and on this." IV. Coquelin on Actors
and Acting. 19th Cent. 21: 800 (Je. '87).

The American Audience. Fortn. 37: 197. Same art. Liv.
Age 164: 730 (Mr. 21, '85).

My Four Favorite Parts. (Hamlet, Richard III., Iago,
and Lear) Forum 16: 33 (S. '93).

Goethe as a Theatre Manager. The. n. s. 13: 11.

Municipal Theatres. The. n. s. 24: 216 (N. '94).

Misconceptions about the Stage. 19th Cent. 32: 670
(O. '92).

(**Irving**, Sir Henry.)   Inspiration and Naturalism in Dramatic
Art.   Educa. 5: 591.
Hamlet and Ophelia.   19th Cent. 1: 513.

Irving's Shylock.   (A. B. MacMahon) Dial (Ch.) 15: 215
(O. 16, '93).

Irving, Miss Isabel, Portrait of.   The. 23: 86 (F. '94).

Italian Drama.   Sat. R. 63: 438.   (W. H. Prescott) No.
Am. 33: 60. No. Am. 5: 182. The. 80, 2: 300. Sat.
R. 63: 84 (Ja. 15, '87).   (R. Davey) Lippinc. 15: 90.
Fraser 26: 236.   Colburn 53: 337; 54: 409.   For.
Quar. R. 27: 1.   (F. Inglis) No. Am. 39: 329.   Blackw.
18: 545; 19: 176; 20: 164; 21: 727; 22: 571: (R. Davey)
No. Am. 19: 90. (C. M. Phillimore) Macmil. 34: 319,
324, 535; 36: 218, 376; 39: 198.   Colburn 53: 337;
54: 409.   Blackw. 53: 551.
Early. (G. E. Mackay) Gent. M. n. s. 20: 478.
Rural.   Sat. R. 63: 84 (Ja. 15, '87).
Modern.   Sat. R. 63: 438.

Italian Stage.   (R. Davey) The. '80, 2: 300.

Italian Tragedy.   Amer. Quar. R. 15: 351. For. Quar. R. 1: 135.
Quart. 24: 72.   Mod. R. 94: 526.   Lon. M. 116: 366.

Jacks, Clara.   The. n. s. 28: 126 (S. '96).

(**Jackson**, Helen Hunt.)   ("H. H.") Ober Ammergau, Village
of. Cent. 3: 663 (M. '83).   Passion Play. Cent. 3: 913
(Ap. '83).

(**Jacox**, F.)   One's First Night at the Play. Colburn 142: 35.
Same art. Liv. Age 96: 735.

Jaeger, Life of Henrik Ibsen.   Quart. 172: 305 (Ap. '91).

James, David.   The. '84, 2: 285, 320.

James, Henry, Jr., at Playwriting.   Sat. R. 78: 662 (D. 15,
'94).

(**James**, Henry, Jr.) The American on the London Stage.
Atlan. 68: 846.

Miss M. E. Braddon. Nation 1 : 593. Same art. Liv. Age
77 : 99.

Coquelin. Cent. 11 : 407.

Dumas, *fils*. New R. (M. '96). N. Y. Herald and Bost.
Herald, Feb. 23, '96.

French Theatre. Galaxy 23 : 437.

Frances Anne Kemble. Temp. Bar 97 : 503 (Jl. '93).

London Theatres. Nation 28 : 400. Galaxy 23 : 661.

Reminiscences of Macready. Nation 20 : 297.

Tommaso Salvini. Atlan. 51 : 377.

"School for Scandal" at the Boston Museum. Atlan.
34 : 754.

Tennyson's "Harold." Nation 24 : 43.

James, Kate. The. n. s. 19 : 197 (Ap. '92).

Janauschek, Mme. Fanny. McClure 3 : 346 (S. '96).

(**Janauschek**, Mme. Fanny.) Eternal Truths of the Drama.
Dr. Mirror 35 : 886 (Xmas, '95).

Japan, Shakspere in. (E. Hausknecht) Poet Lore 1 : 466
(O. '89).

Theatre Days in. (Georgia Cayvan) Dr. Mirror 37 : 939
(Xmas, '96).

Japanese Ballet. Potter Am. Mo. 15 : '96.

Japanese Play. Belgra. 86 : 359 (S. '95).

Japanese Theatre. (T. J. Nakagawa) Scrib. 7 : 603 (My.
'90). (J. C. W. Parr) The. '84, 2 : 184. (E. B. Rodgers)
Outing 25 : 191 (D. '94). (E. R. Scudmore) Cosmop.
10 : 685. All the Year 38 : 40. Appleton 2 : 449, 481.
Galaxy 21 : 75.

A Day in. (E. H. House) Atlan. 30 : 257. Same art.
Cornh. 26 : 341.

Japanese Theatres. Eng. Dom. M. 17 : 186.

Chinese and. (L. Wingate) Murray 2 : 89, 232.

(**Jastrow**, M. Jr.) "Moving wood" in "Macbeth," Arabic
   version of. Poet Lore 2: 247.
   Shylock. Penn Mo. 11: 725.

Jefferson, Joseph. (M. Bacheller) Munsey 12: 497 (F.'95).
   (J. B. Runnion) Lippinc. 4: 167 (Ag.'69). (J. R.
   Towse) Cent. 5: 476 (Ja.'84). (Wm. Winter) Har-
   per 73: 391 (Ag.'86).
   As Rip Van Winkle. Ev. Sat. 10: 153, 162. (S. John-
   son) Radical 6: 133. (A. G. Sedgwick) Nation 9: 247.
   (L. C. Davis) Atlan. 19: 750. Appleton 19: 146. O.
   and N. 2: 684. (L. C. Davis) Lippinc. 24: 57. Scrib.
   1: 216 (D. '70). Harper 42: 614 (Ap. '71). (G. A.
   Pierce) Atlan. 52: 695.
   At Home. (W. H. Ballou) Cosmop. 7: 121.
   at the Normal College. Critic 27: 284 (N. 2, '95).
   Autobiography of, Review of. (B. Matthews) Nation
   51: 386. (J. B. Runnion) Dial (Ch.) 11: 237.
   Birthplace of. (W. S. Hale) Dr. Mirror 35: 886.
   (Xmas, '95).
   in "The Rivals." Scrib. 22: 183 (D. '80).
   Winter's Life of. Dial (Ch.) 17: 256 (N. 1,'94).

(**Jefferson**, Joseph). Autobiography. Cent. 17: 3, 184, 367,
   494, 643, 803; 18: 135, 263, 406, 538, 704, 814 (N.'89
   to O.'90).
   Edwin Booth. Critic 25: 210 (S. 29, '94).
   Success on the Stage. No. Am. 135: 580 (D.'82).

Jeffries, Maud. The. n. s. 27: 156 (Mr.'96).

(**Jeffrey**, F.) Hazlitt on the Characters of Shakspere. Ed. R.
   28: 472.

Jeffrey, J., and Wm. Hazlitt. Blackw. 3: 303.

(**Jennings**, H. J.) Irving as King Lear. Gent. M. n. s. 49:
   624 (D.'92).
   "King Lear" at the Lyceum. Gent. M. n. s. 49: 624,
   634 (D.'92).
   "King Lear," Famous Actors in. Gent. M. n. s. 49:
   509 (N.'92).

(**Jenkin**, Fleeming.) Mrs. Siddons as Lady Macbeth. 19th
    Cent. 3 : 296 (F. '78).

(**Jerrold**, E.) Dumas, *fils.* Temp. Bar 54 : 392.
    French Drama of To-day. Gent. M. n. s. 12 : 704.

Jews, Stage. Sat. R. 62 : 451. *See also " Shylock," " Merchant of Venice," etc.*

Jewett, on the Drama. Spec. 59 : 873.

Joan of Arc, Bernhardt as. Critic 19 : 269.

(**Johnson**, L.) Plays of Michael Field. Acad. 38 : 123.
    R. L. Stevenson as a Dramatist. Acad. 43 : 473 (Je. 3,'93).

(**Johnson**, R. B.) Books about Ibsen. Acad. 45 : 285 (Ap. 7,'94).

(**Johnson**, S.) J. Jefferson as Rip Van Winkle. Radical 6 : 133.

(**Johnson**, C. P.) Dramatic Adaptations of the Works of
    Thackeray. Ath. '92, 2 : 107, 171 (Jl. & Ag.).

Johnson, Dr., and Garrick. No. Am. 4 : 38.

(**Johnson**, C. F.) King John and Richard II. N. Eng. M.45 : 219.

Jonson, Ben. Brit. Quar. R. 25 : 285.

(**Johnston**, Richard Malcolm). Delicacy of Shakspere. Cath.
    World 39 : 119. Tragic Lovers of Shakspere, Cath.
    World 40 : 84.

Jones, Henry Arthur. The. 86, 2 : 132, 174. (J. A. Hamilton)
    Munsey 11 : 174 (My. '94).
    " Dancing Girl." Sat. R. 71 : 99.
    " Dancing Girl," Moral Purpose in. (J. D. Hunting) The.
        n. s. 18 : 121 (Mr. '92).
    " Hard Hit." (E. A. Bendall) The. n. s. 8 : 99.
    " Judah." Sat. R. 69 : 640. (F. Wedmore) Acad. 37 :
        396. Harper 73 : 478 (Ag. '86).
    Play-Making. Sat. R. 72 : 690 (D. 19, '91).
    " Renaissance of the Drama." Quart. 182 : 399 (O. '95).
        (Chas. Dickens, 2nd) The. n. s. 25 : 322 (Je. '95).
    " Saints and Sinners." (H. Norman) Nation 39 : 371.

13

(**Jones**, Henry Arthur.) Author. Dr. Mirror 23: 590 (Ap. 19, '90).

> The Bible and the Stage. New R. (F. '93).
> Can we have an Ideal Theatre? Young Man (Mr. '93).
> First Night Judgment of Plays. 19th Cent. 26: 43 (Jl. '89).
> Future of the English Drama. New. R. 9: 177 (Ag. '93).
> Literary Drama. (Reply to II. D. Traill) New R. (Ja. '92).
> Outlook of Drama, 1885. Eng. Illust. 2: 280, 341.
> Dr. Pearson on the Modern Drama. 19th Cent. 34: 543 (O. '93).
> A Playwright's Grumble. To-day (D. '84).
> Religion and the Stage. 19th Cent. (Ja. '95).
> Science of the Drama. New R. 5: 83.
> Theatre and the Mob. 19th Cent. 14: 441 (S. '83).

(**Jones**, II. K.) The "Tempest." J. Spec. Philos. 9: 293.

(**Jones**, M. C.) Eleanora Duse. Critic 26: 67, 117 (F. 4, 25, '93).

(**Jones**, W. W.) Thos. W. Robertson. The. '79, 1: 355.

Juliet. Eng. Dom. M. 16: 278. (O. Thorpe) The. n. s. 22: 353 (N.'93). (Lady Martin) Blackw. 131: 141. Same art. Liv. Age 152: 245, 738.
> Mary Anderson as. *See "Mary Anderson."*
> Modjeska as. *See "Modjeska."*

Juliets, Some Famous. (H. B. Baker) Gent. M. n. s. 33: 594. (B. Sturgess) Peterson n. s. 6: 1065 (O.'96).

Juliets of the Stage. (M. Aldrich) Nickell 6: 348 (D.'96).
> *See also "Romeo and Juliet," "Shakspere," etc.*

"**Julius** Caesar." (D. J. Snider) Western 2: 38, 77. Same art. J. Spec. Philos. 6: 234. Blackw. 37: 747. (W. J. Rolfe) Poet Lore 6: 7 (Ja. '94).

(**Jusseraud**, J. J.) Drama of the Middle Ages. Chaut. 19: 65 (Ap.'94).

Kean, Chas. (T. P. Grinstead) Bentley 42: 209. (D. Cook)
Gent. M. n. s. 25: 712. Dub. Univ. 36: 412. Same
art. Ecl. M. 21: 538. Ev. Sat. 5: 251.
and the Modern Stage. Ev. Sat. 5: 552.
Life and Times of. Fraser 60: 361. New Q. 8: 285.

Kean, Edmund. Harper 24: 72; 61: 875 (N.'75); 69: 59.
(T. W. Clark) Knick. 3: 101; 6: 216. Blackw. 3:
77; 16: 271; 38: 71. Quart. 54: 109. Ann. Register
8: 438. Chamb. J. 46: 423. Temp. Bar 49: 180.
Same art. Ecl. M. 88: 414. Same art. Liv. Age 132: 668.
and John Kemble. (T. Martin) 19th Cent. 7: 291. Ecl.
M. 94: 542.
as King Lear. Lon. M. 1: 686.
Early Days of. Fraser 7: 734; 8: 499. Colburn 40: 434.
Life of. Quart. 54: 109. Mod. R. 137: 348.
My Acquaintance with. (T. C. Grattan) Colburn 39: 7,
143.
Recollections of. Colburn 41: 51.
Portrait of, at the Garrick Club. The. n. s. 26: 71 (Ag.
'95).

Kean's Monument to Cooke. Harper 44: 188 (Ja.'72).

(Keeler, R.) Three Years a Negro Minstrel. Atlan. 24: 71.

Keeley, Mrs., and the Queen. The. n. s. 25: 198 (Ap.'95).

Keeleys, The. (W. D. Adams) The. n. s. 26: 328 (D.'95).

(Kelly, J. G.) Falstaff. Overland 13: 352.

Kemble, Chas. Harper 44: 188.

Kemble, Frances Anne (Fanny), (Mrs. Butler). Galaxy 6:
797. Internat. M. 1: 310. Liv. Age 139: 628. Appleton
21: 273. Harper 24: 75; 30: 394; 59: 72. Temp.
Bar 66: 172. Same art. Ecl. M. 100: 104. Temp. Bar
102: 326 (Jl.'94). (H. Lee) Atlan. 71: 662 (My.'93).
(MacMahon) Belgra. 80: 373 (Ap.'93). Same art. Liv.
Age 197: 692 (Je. 10,'93). (Mrs. Ritchie) Macmil. 68:
190 (Jl.'93). (II. James) Temp. Bar 97: 503 (Jl.'93).
Sat. R. 75: 67 (Ja. 21, '93). The. '79, 1: 224.

Kemble, Frances Anne (Fanny), (Mrs. Butler). "American Journal." Tait n. s. 2: 465.

and her Critics. Fraser 12: 327.

at Lenox. (C. B. Todd) Lippinc. 52: 66 (Jl.'93).

Death of. Critic 22: 372 (Mr.'93).

"Journal." Quart. 54: 39. Mod. R. 137: 402.

"Plays." Liv. Age 80: 118.

First Appearance of. (P. Fitzgerald) The. '86, 2: 117.

"Journal in America." Quart. 54: 39. So. Lit. Mess. 1: 524. (A. H. Everett) No. Am. 41: 109. Am. Mo. M. 5: 280. Ed. R. 61: 379.

"Record of Girlhood." Quart. 154: 83 (Jl. '82). (B. Murphy) Cath. World 30: 334. Internat. R. 6: 589. Penn. M. 10: 231.

"Record of Later Life." Sat. R. 54: 56. Spec. 55: 595. Lit. World (Bost.) 13: 310. Ath. '82, 2: 39. Quart. 154: 83 (Jl.'82). Same art. Liv. Age 154: 707. Lippinc. 30: 442 (O. '82). (G. T. Lanigan) Amer. 4: 266.

Moral Element in "Records etc." (I. F. Bellows) Univ. R. 19: 115.

(Kemble, Frances Anne). Autobiographical Recollections. Atlan. 36: 152, 722; 37: 76, 711; 38: 32, 705; 39: 73, 432.

On the Stage. Harper 28: 364 (F. '64).

T. Salvini in "Othello." Temp. Bar 71: 368.

Notes on Shakspere. Spec. 56: 53. Blackw. 1: 455. Atlan. 6: 288.

Mrs. Siddons. Harper 28: 364 (F.'64).

Notes on the Characters of "Macbeth." Macmil. 16: 76. Same art. Liv. Age 93: 523.

Lady Macbeth. Macmil. 17: 354.

Queen Katharine and Wolsey in "King Henry VIII." Lippinc. 16: 685.

Differences of Dramatic and Theatrical. Cornh. 8: 733.

(**Kennedy**, H. A.)   A Dialogue on the Drama.   19th Cent.
  38 : 322 (Ag. '95).
   Drama of the Moment.   19th Cent. 30 : 258 (Ag. '91).

(**Kent**, P.)   The Funeral of Molière.   The. n. s. 11 : 296.

"**King** Arthur " on the Stage.   (Henry Elliot) The. n. s. 24 :
  169 (O. '94).   *See " Comyns Carr."*

"**King** Edward II."   (K. Elze) Ath. '87, 1 : 491.   (B. G.
  Kinnear) Ath. '87, 1 : 521.   (B. Nicholson) Ath. '87,
  1 : 554.

King Henry IV. and Falstaff on the Stage.   (F. Hawkins)
  The. n. s. 27 : 211 (Ap. '96).

"**King** Henry IV."   (D. J. Snider) Western 3 : 344, 396,
  447.   (T. P. Courtenay) Colburn 54 : 42.   Blackw.
  39 : 699.   (R. L. Ashhurst) Poet Lore 1 : 367.

"**King** Henry V."   (D. J. Snider) Western 3 : 541.   (T. P.
  Courtenay) Colburn 54 : 251.   All the Year 43 : 510.

"**King** Henry VI."   (T. P. Courtenay) Colburn 54 : 375, 494;
  55 : 57.

"**King** Henry VI. Part I."   Knowl. 11 : 244.

"**King** Henry VIII."   (T. P. Courtenay) Colburn 55 : 346.
  Gent. M. n. s. 48 : 214 (F. '92) ; 427 (Ap. '92).
   at the Lyceum Theatre.   (F. Wedmore) Acad. 41 : 70
  (Jan. 16, '92).
   On the Stage (F. Hawkins) Eng. Illust. 9 : 291 (Ja. '92).
   (R. W. Lowe and W. Archer) Longm. 19 : 249, 624, 634
  (Ja. '92).
   Characters of Queen Katharine and Cardinal Wolsey.
  (F. A. Kemble) Lipp. 16 : 685.

"**King** John."   (D. J. Snider) Western 3 : 89, 157.   (T. P.
  Courtenay) Colburn 53 : 250.   All the Year 49 : 222.
   at Oxford.   Sat. R. 71 : 195.
   and " Richard II."   (C. F. Johnson) N. Eng. M. 45 : 219.

Knowles, James Sheridan, Sonnets to. (Charles Lamb) Lon.
M. 2: 302.
"Virginius." Lon. M. 1: 692.
Visit to Cork. New Eng. M. 8: 63.
"Woman's Wit." (Comedy). Dub. R. 5: 229. Mod. R.
146: 326.

(Kobbé, Gustav.) Behind the Scenes of an Opera House.
Scrib. 4: 435 (O. '88).

(Koener, S.) Hamlet as a Solar Myth. Poet Lore 3: 214.

(Kalisch, L.) Claque in Paris Theatres. Ev. Sat. 5: 102.

(Lacy, Henry.) Fact and Fiction about Shakspere. The. n. s.
25: 88 (F. '95).

(Lacy, J.) Theatricals of Our Day, (1824). Lon. M. 10: 635.

Lady Macbeth. (F. A. Kemble) Macmil. 17: 354. Same
art. Liv. Age 97: 724. Ecl. M. 70: 481. (G. C. Bibb)
Western 1: 287. Portf. (Den.) 11: 238. (J. A. St.
John) Ecl. M. 16: 202. Ev. Sat. 5: 242. (R. Munro)
J. Spec. Philos. 21: 30.
Bernhardt as. Sat. R. 57: 777. Same art. Critic 5: 8.
Charlotte Cushman as. (G. F. Ferris) Lakeside 7: 407.
See "Cushman."
Modjeska as. Poet Lore 4: 42 (Ja. 92). *See "Modjeska."*
Mrs. Siddons as. (Fleeming Jenkin) 19th Cent. 3: 296
(F. '78).

"Lady of Lyons." *See "Lytton."*

(Laidlaw, F. A.) How to Write Dramas for Music. The.
n. s. 18: 67.

(Laird, Louis K. R.) H. Ibsen's Merits and Defects. New
Bohemian 2: 251 (Je. '96).

(Lamb, Charles.) Old Actors. Lon. Mod. 5: 174, 305; 6: 349.
Imperfect Dramatic Illusion. Lon. M. 12: 599.
Sonnets to James Sheridan Knowles. Lon. M. 2: 302.
Criticism of Passages of "The Tempest." Lon. M. 8:
492.

14

(**Lamb**, Lady.) Early Life of Colley Cibber. The. '79, 1 : 92.

(**Lamphigh**, G. W.) In a Chinese Theatre. Macmil. 57 : 36.

(**Lancaster**, A. E.) Edwin Forrest. Potter Am. Mo. 8 : 161.

American Drama. Potter Am. Mo. 8 : 23, 346.

(**Lang**, Andrew.) J. B. P. Molière. Scrib. 9 : 725.

"As You Like It." Harper 82 : 3.

"Comedy of Errors." Harper 82 : 550.

"Measure for Measure." Harper 84 : 62.

"Merchant of Venice." Harper 80 : 355.

"Merry Wives of Windsor." Harper 80 : 3.

"Much Ado About Nothing." Harper 83 : 489.

"The Taming of the Shrew." Harper 90 : 89 (D. '94).

"Winter's Tale." Harper 88 : 710 (Ap. '94).

"Tempest." Harper 84 : 653 (Ap. '92).

(**Langel**, A.) French Drama. Nation 34 : 51. " Princess of Bagdad," " Denise," " Francillon." *See "Dumas, fils."* "Théodora," "Georgette," "Madame Sans Gêne." *See " Victorien Sardou."*

Langtry, Mrs. Lillian. The. '82, 1 : 65, 113; '82, 2 : 233.

as an Actress. Sat. R. 54: 441. Spec. 55 : 1507.

as Cleopatra. (C. Howard) The. n. s. 16 : 287.

as Pauline. The.'85, 1 : 1. (P. Fitzgerald) '86, 1 : 221.

as Rosalind. The. n. s. 13 : 210. Sat. R. 69 : 258.

at Manchester. (W. D. Adams) The. '83, 2 : 136.

(**Lanigan**, G. L.) Modern Dramatists. Amer. 3 : 89.

Fanny Kemble's Records of Later Life. Amer. 4 : 266.

(**Latham**, R. G.) Pyrrhus and Hecuba in "Hamlet." Ev. Sat. 11 : 539.

"Titus Andronicus." Fraser 82 : 361.

(**Lathe**, A. M.) "Midsummer Night's Dream." Educa. 12 : 406 (My. '92).

"Two Gentlemen of Verona." Acad. (Syr.) 7 : 24 (F. '92.)

(**Lathrop,** Geo. P.) Personality and Situations in Plays. Dr.
 Mirror 23: 587 (M 29, '90).

 Author and Theatre. Dr. Mirror 24: 600 (Je. 28, '90).

(**Lathrop,** H. B.) "Hamlet." Acad. (Syr.) 7: 89 (Mr. '92).

(**Lathrop,** Lorin A.) A Day with Mr. Willard. The. n. s.
 23: 59 (F. '94).

"**La Tosca.**" *See " Victorien Sardou,"* etc.

Launce and his Dog. (J. C. Lockhart) Manch. 2, 1 : 86.

(**Lawhead,** L. D.) Was Falstaff Immoral? Poet Lore 3 :
 142.

(**Lawler,** H. D.) Molière the Dramatist. Poet Lore (Ap.'96).

Lawrence, Everetta. The. '86, 1 : 59.

 American Actors in England. Gent. M. n. s. 46: 82.

(**Lawrence,** W. J.) Stage Falstaffs. Gent. M. n. s. 42:
 425.

 Genesis of Pantomime. The. n. s. 25 : 28 (Ja. '95).

 Pantomime in U. S. The. n. s. 27: 83 (F. '96).

 Sensation Scenes. Gent. M. n. s. 37 : 400.

 Stage Ghosts. Gent. M. n. s. 39 : 545. Same art. Ecl.
 M. 110: 210.

 English Players in Paris. Gent. M. n. s. 45: 446.

Laws affecting the Theatre. (R. V. Rodgers) Green Bag 6 :
 259, 321, 376 (Je., Jl. and Ag. '94).

(**Lazarus,** Emma.) T. Salvini. Cent. 1 : 110 (N. '81).

 T. Salvini as Lear. Cent. 4: 88 (Mr. '83).

Lea, Marion. The. n. s. 19: 202 (Ap. '92).

Leading Men of the Present Day. (W. D. Adams) The. n. s.
 22: 24 (Jl. '93).

(**Leahy,** W. A.) Stage Conditions of English Drama. Harv.
 Mo. 6: 207.

 English Elizabethan Theatre. Harv. Mo. 6: 207.

(**Le Clercq,** Theodore). Proverbes Dramatiques. Lon. M.
 12: 17.

(**Lee,** R.) Epitome of the Drama. The. '86, 2: 258.

(**Lee,** S. R.) Original of Shylock. Gent. M. n. s. 24: 185.

(**Lee,** H.) Frances Anne Kemble. Atlan. 71: 662 (My. '93).

Lee, Nathaniel. (M. E. Wotton). The. '86, 2: 76.

(**Lee,** Vernon). The Dramatic and the Undramatic. Contemp. 50: 239 (Ag. '86).

Leg Business. (Oliver Logan) Galaxy 4: 440.

Legouvé, E. Spec. 71: 402 (S. 23, '93).

(**Leifchild,** F.) Hamlet. Contemp. 43: 31.

Leighton, Margaret. The. '81, 1: 321, 343.

Lemaître, Fred'k. (C. Barrère) Gent. M. n. s. 13: 447. (W. Sikes) Lippinc. 15: 588 (My. '75). Lond. Soc. 9: 552. (J. W. Sherer) Gent. M. n. s. 36: 147. Ecl. M. 106: 467. Lond. Soc. 39: 155.
Robert Macaire and Ruy Blas. Temp. Bar 62: 537. Sat. R. 55: 467.

Lemaître, Jules. Sat. R. 79: 857 (Je. 29, '95).

(**Lemon,** M.) Actors' Holiday. Ev. Sat. 4: 747.

(**Lenning,** T.) "Macbeth." Penn Mo. 1: 172.

(**Leppington,** C. H.) Work and Wages Behind the Scenes. National 17: 245 (Ap. '91).

Leslie, Fanny. The. '82, 1: 193, 218.
Miss. Recollection of Charles Mathews. Godey 31: 6.

Lessing and the German Drama. (W. L. Phelps) N. Eng. M. 51: 198.
Dramatic Notes. Macmil. 57: 488.

(**Lestocq,** W.) Actors' Association. The. n. s. 24: 298 (D. '94).

Levey, the Sisters. The. n. s. 24: 56 (Ag. '94).

Lewes, Geo. H., and the Stage. (W. Archer) Fortn. (F. '96). (A. Trollope) Fortn. 31: 18. Same art. Liv. Age. 140: 307. Nature 19: 106. Pop. Sci. Mo. 9: 743. (G. M. Towle) Appleton 5: 133. Peop. J. 10: 323.
as a Dramatic Critic. (W. D. Adams) The. n. s. 27: 337 (Je. '96).

(**Lewes**, Geo. H.) "On Actors and Acting." Lippinc. 31 :
647 (My. '78).
Authors and Managers. Westm. 37: 71.
French Criticisms of Shakspere. Cornh. 11 : 33, 256.
French Drama. Westm. 34: 287. Cornh. 11 : 33.
Classifying Theatres. Ed. R. 78: 382 (O. '43).
Theatres and Dramatic Reform. Ed. R. 78: 382.
Recent Tragedies. Westm. 37: 321.

(**Lewis**, A.) Henry Irving. Dub. Univ. 90: 284.

Lewis, James. (L. Richardson) Metrop. 4: 341 (D. '96).

(**Lewis**, Tayler.) Influences of the Theatres. Harper 5 :
406 (Ag. '52).

(**Leyland**, J.) Henry Irving. Amer. 6: 312; 7: 122, 141.

Libretti, Lyric Drama and. (S. J. A. Fitz-Gerald) The. n. s.
20: 161 (O. '92).

Librettist, the Good. The. n. s. 13: 241.

License, Dramatic. (W. G. Wills) The. '80, 1 : 199.

(**Lillie**, J.) Helena Modjeska. Temp. Bar 66 : 22, 551; 67:
73.

Linden, Laura. The. '85, 2 : 233, 281.

Linden, Marie. The. '83, 2 : 162.

Lindley, Henrietta. The. '86, 2 : 117, 173.

(**Linton**, Mrs. Lynn.) The Stage as a Profession for Women.
National 5 : 8 (Mr. '85).

(**Lippman**, von, E. O.) Ignorance of Shakspere. New R. 4 :
250.

(**Lipscomb**, A. A.) Hamlet, a Psychological Study. Meth.
R. 44: 665.

Literature and the Drama. (E. Fawcett) Dial (Ch.) 14 :
38. (H. D. Traill) New R. 5: 502. (G. Moore)
Fortn. 52: 620 (D. '89). Poet Lore 2: 33 (Ja. '90).
(F. Marshall) The. '78, 2: 23.

Literature and the Stage. (Earl Lytton) Fortn. 40: 12, 215.
Same art. Ecl. M. 101: 501, 658.
and the Stage, Divorce between. (Alfred Austin) National
2: 680 (Ja. '84).
on the Stage. Dial (Ch.) 13: 336 (D. '92).
American Dramatic, Beginnings of. (P. L. Ford) N.
Eng. M. n. s. 9: 673 (F. 9, '94).
Dramatic, Extracts from. (G. Moore) Poet Lore 2: 33
(Ja. '90).
Dramatic, Geoffrey on. (A. H. Everett) No. Am. 10:
291. Am. Q. 8: 134. Westm. 18: 31. Lon. M. 22:
298. So. R. 16: 377.
Ward on English Dramatic. (W. B. Donne) Macmil.
33: 314.
Dramatic, in 1869. Colburn 146: 92.
and the Drama. Mod. R. 129: 461. Fraser 41: 69.
Dramatic. (Lady Pollock) Temp. Bar 44: 331.

Literary Drama, Mr. Pinero and. The n. s. 22: 3 (Jl. '93).
Plays, the Productions of. (H. B. Tree) Fortn. 54:
925.

(Littledale, H.) Cymbeline in a Hindu Drama. Macmil. 42:
65. Same art. Liv. Age 145: 695.

(Littlejohn, J.) Playwriting. Irish Mo. 17: 356.

Living Pictures. New R. 11: 461 (N. '94).

Lloyd, Robt. The Poet of Acting. (W. D. Adams) The.
'79, 2: 78.

(Lloyd, W. W.) Emendations in Shakspere. Ath. '84, 1:
727.
"Romeo and Juliet." Ath. '84, 2: 402.
"Measure for Measure." Ath. '83, 1: 636.

(Lockhart, J. C.) Launce and His Dog. Manch. Q. 1: 86.

(Logan, Olive.) Grand Old Days of Histrionics. Harper 69:
48 (Je. '79).
Secret Regions of the Stage. Harper 48: 629 (Ap. '74).

(**Logan,** Olive.) Leg Business. Galaxy 4: 440.

    American and Foreign Theatres. Galaxy 5: 22.

    Drunken Drama. Galaxy 4: 934.

    Grand Days of English Stage. Harper 59: 48.

London and Actors (W. Thornbury). Belgra. 7: 360, 546;
    8: 70, 230, 394; 10: 104, 248, 512.

    County Councils and the Theatres. (Chas. Dickens 2nd.)
    The. n. s. **25**: 140 (Mr. '95).

    County Council and Theatre. The. n. s. 24: 105 (S.
    '94).

    at the Old Globe Theatre. (W. H. Hudson) The. n.
    s. **15**: 173.

    Drama. Fraser 71: 124. Fraser 38: 41. Blackw. **2**:
    426, 567, 664; 3: 77, 207, 329; 4: 443, 708; 5: 71,
    317; 6: 51, 624; 7: 182, 307. *See also "English
    Drama."*

    Stage, the American on the. (H. James, Jr.) Atlan. 68:
    846.

    Theatre. (H. F. Randolph) N. Eng. M. n. s. 10: 318
    (My. '94).

    Theatre, First, in. (R. Bell) Once a Week 1: 464. Same
    art. Liv. Age 64: 249.

    Theatres. (T. P. Grinstead) Bentley 35: 489, 541; 36:
    89, 371. (H. James, Jr.) Galaxy 23: 661. Blackw. 71:
    460, 596. (H. James) Nation 28: 400. Scrib. 21:
    354. Dark Blue 2: 761. Broadw. 6: 283. Mus. 9:
    247. Scrib. 21: 354 (Ja. '81). (G. Turner) The. n. s.
    14: 65.

    Theatres and their Plays. Temp. Bar 38: 256; 39: 547.

    Theatres, In. (A. B. Walkley) Cosmopolis 4: 74 (O. '96).

    Ordish's Early Theatres. Sat. R. 78: 462 (O. 27, '94).

    Season of '90 and '91. (W. D. Adams) The. n. s. 18:
    53.

    the Minor Theatres of. (P. Egan) Atlan. 25: 294.

    Theatres, Outlook of, 1892. Sat. R. 74: 220.

"**London** Assurance." *See " Boucicault."*

(**Lytton,** Robert Lytton Bulwer, Earl of Lytton.) Garrick as
Hamlet. Fortn. 15 : 221, 352 (F. and Mr. '71). Same
art. Liv. Age 109 : 67, 236.
Stage in Relation to Literature. Fortn. 40 : 12, 215.
Same art. Ecl. M. 101 : 501, 658.

Macaire, Robert, the New. (Rich'd Davey) The. n. s. 26 : 30
(Jl. '95).

(**Macaulay,** Thomas Babington.) Comic Dramatists of the
Restoration. Ed. R. 72 : 49. Mus. 42 : 31.

Macbeth and David. Mo. Rel. M. 37 : 117.
as the Celtic Type. (M. O'Neill) Blackw. 150 : 376.
and Lady Macbeth. (P. W. Clayden) Fortn. 8 : 153.
Considered as a Celt. (J. D. Montgomery) National
13 : 181.

"**Macbeth.**" (J. E. Murdoch) Forum 10 : 72 (S. '90). (J.
Coleman) Gent. M. n. s. 42 : 218. (H. N. Hudson)
Am. Whig R. 6 : 581. Westm. 41 : 1. Blackw. 63 :
292. Fraser 22 : 613; 23 : 295; 24 : 401; 25 : 81.
(E. F. Mosby) So. M. 9 : 348. (T. Lenning) Penn
Mo. 1 : 172. (My. '70). (F. A. Kemble) Macmil.
16 : 76. Same art. Liv. Age 93 : 523. Cornh. 59 :
133.
Analysis of Motive in. Foster Mo. Ref. 1 : 47.
and Common Sense. (W. Archer) Murray 5 : 182.
Controversy about. (F. Thompson) Dub. R. 105 : 140.
(D. J. Snider) Western 1 : 557, 601. Cornh. 32 : 577.
(J. A. Heraud) Peop. J. 8 : 69, 78, 89. (D. Cook)
Once a Week 12 : 380.
Criticism and Acting of. (G. Fletcher) Westm. 41 : 1.
Distortions of, The English Stage. Nat. R. 17 : 292.
Ethics of. Dub. Univ. 65 : 280.
Fletcher's studies in. Sat. R. 67 : 391.
Irving's Production of. Sat. R. 67 : 373. Spec. 62 : 9.
(F. Wedmore) Acad. 35 : 14.

15

"**Macbeth**," Milton's objection to the treatment of.   (J. W. Hales) 19th Cent. 30: 319.
 Morals and Metaphysics of. (C. Turner). The n. s. 14: 1.
 Morality of. New Eng. M. 1: 297.
 "Moving wood" in, Arabic version of. (M. Jastrow, Jr.) Poet Lore 2: 247.
 Music of. Ev. Sat. 9: 263.
 On the Stage. All the Year 35: 52. (W. Archer and R. W. Lowe) Eng. Illust. 6: 233. (F. Hawkins) The. n. s. 12: 281; 13: 1.
 Retzsch's Outlines of. For. Quart. R. 12: 445.
 Revival of. Chamb. J. 19: 214.
 Sensational Notice of. All the Year 11: 115.
 Studies in. (A. H. Tolman) Atlan. 69: 241 (F. '92).
 Supernatural in. (W. Townsend) Canad. Mo. 3: 199 (Jl. '94).
 Third Murderer in. (H. Irving) 19th Cent. 1: 327.
 True Tale of. Chamb. J. 2: 40.
 With Kelly's Music. (A. A. Wheeler) Overland n. s. 7: 185.

(**MacCarthy**, John.) Use and Abuse of the Stage. Cath. World 15: 836 (S. '72).

(**MacDonald**, R. C.) Insanity of Hamlet. Acad. (Syr.) 7: 29 (F. '92).

(**Mackail**, J. W.) "Becket." Acad. 26: 421.

(**MacKay**, G. E.) Early Italian Drama. Gent. M. n. s. 20: 478.

 Macklin, Charles. Irish Dramatist. Irish Q. 3: 857. Temp. Bar 52: 173.

(**MacMahon**, A. B.) Henry Irving's Shylock. Dial (Ch.) 15: 215 (O. 16, '93).

(**MacMahon**, E.) Frances Anne Kemble. Belgra. 80: 373 (Ap. '93).

Maeterlinck, Maurice. (W. Archer) Fortn. 56 : 346. (R. Burton) Atlan. 74 : 672 (N. '94). Poet Lore 5 : 151 (Mr. '93). (R. Hovey) 19th Cent. 37 : 491 (Mr. '95). (J. Heard, Jr.) Critic 20 : 354 (Je. 25, '92). (J. Sharp) Acad. 41 : 270 (Mr. 19, '92).

Plays of. Spec. 69 : 455 (O. 1, '92).

"Princess Maline" and "The Intruder." Ath. '92, 1 : 525 (Ap. 23, '92).

Maid Marian on the Stage. (A. B. Walkley) The. n. s. 19 : 277 (My. '92).

(Maitland, J. A. Fuller.) Falstaff and the New Italian Opera. 19th Cent. 33 : 803 (My. '93).

Incidental Music in Plays. The. n. s. 25 : 200 (Ap. '95).

Musical Instruments as Stage "Props." The. n. s. 26 : 269 (N. '95).

(Malcomb, E. H.) Theatrical Retrospections. Sharpe 46 : 116 ; 47 : 150.

(Mallock, W. H.) A Socialist in a Corner Fortn. 61 : 693 (My. '94).

(Malone, John.) The Actor, the Manager, and the Public. Forum 20 : 235 (O. '95).

An Actor's Memory of Edwin Booth. Forum 15 : 594. (Jl. '93).

Booth, the Elder, A Memento of. Dr. Mirror 37 : 939. (Xmas, '96).

Catholic View of Shakspere. Cath. World 55 : 716 (Ag. '92).

The House of "The Players." Dr. Mirror 35 : 886. (Xmas, '95).

Shakspere and the Church. Seminary 1 : 8, 9, 11 (Jl. '93).

Management. Actor Management. Gent. M. n. s. 47 : 320 (H. A. Jones and H. B. Tree) Fortn. 54 : 1. Sat. R. 67 : 276 ; 69 : 767, 795 ; 70 : 168. (Stephen Fiske) Dr. Mirror, 24 : 601 (Jl. 5, '90).

Management. Actor Managers. (Bram Stoker, Henry Irving, Charles Wyndham) 19th Cent. **26:** 1040 (Je.'90).
Author Managers. Gent. M. n. s. **47:** 535.
The Actor Management and the Dramatist. (Lady Pollock) Temp. Bar **44:** 33.

Manager, the Actor, the, and the Public. (John Malone) Forum **20:** 235 (O.'95).
Leaves from Portfolio of a. (J. W. (Cole) Calcraft) Dub. Univ. **36:** 656 (D. '50); **37:** 217, 720 (F. and Je. '51); **38:** 39, 272 (Jl. and S. '51); **39:** 423, 564, 679 (Ap. My. and Je. '51).

Managers, Actors and, under Queen Anne. (G. A. Aitken) Ath. '88, **2:** 203, 267.
of Drury Lane from Killegrew to Harris. (P. H. Fitzgerald) The. n. s. **9:** 28, 295.
Actors as. Sat. R. **67:** 276; **69:** 767, 795; **70:** 168.
Policy of our Leading. (W. A. L. Bettany) The. n. s. **22:** 182 (Ap.'94).

Manager's Note-Book. Colburn **51:** 485, 530; **52:** 63, 323; **53:** 101, 530; **54:** 87, 457.

Mannerism. (D. Cook) The. '79, **1:** 165.

Mansfield, Richard, on Staten Island. Harper **83:** 149 (Je. '91).
as Richard III. (C. Porter) Poet Lore **2:** 30 (Ja. '90). Sat. R. **67:** 341, 406.

(Mansfield, Richard.) Concerning Acting. No. Am. **197:** 337 (S.'94).
A Plain Talk on the Drama. No. Am. **155:** 308 (S.'92).

(March, F. A.) "As You Like It." Nation **52:** 202.
"Tempest." Nation **55:** 112 (Ag. 11, '92).

(Marie, C.) My Acquaintance with Rachel. Harper **16:** 805 (My.'58).

Marie Antoinette and the Stage. (F. Hawkins) The. n. s. **28:** 80 (Ag.'96).

(**Marguerites**, Mme. de)   C. Cushman and Rachel.   Sharpe
    15 : 13.

Marlowe, Christopher, and his Times.   (E. Norton) Harv.
    Mo. 1 : 50.
    "Doctor Faustus."   Blackw. 1 : 388.   Temp. Bar 98 :
        515.
    "Edward II."   Blackw. 2 : 27.
    "Jew of Malta."   Blackw. 2 : 260.
    "Tamburlane the Great."   (F. Rogers) Acad. 34 : 244.

Marlowe, Julia.   *See "Mrs. Julia Marlowe Taber."*
    as Rosalind.   Poet Lore 1 : 141.

(**Marricott**, Thos.)   Legal Status of the Actor.   The. n. s.
    25 : 260 (My.'95).

(**Marshall**, A. F.)   Spirit of Gilbert's Comedies.   Month 55 :
    254.

(**Marshall**, F. H.)   Daly's Company in "The Taming of
    the Shrew."   The. n. s. 12 : 10.
    Wills' "Faust" at the Lyceum.   The. '86, 1 : 59.
    Thomas Heywood.   The. n. s. 9 : 205.

(**Marshall**, E.)   The Dramatic Season.   McClure 4 : 179 (Ja.
    '95).

(**Marston**, W.)   Helena Modjeska in England.   Critic 1 : 144.

(**Martin**, Lady : Helen Faucit).   Some of Shakspere's Characters.
    Beatrice.   Blackw. 137 : 203.   Same art. Liv. Age 164 :
        602 (M. 7, '85).
    Juliet.   Blackw. 131 : 31, 141.   Same art. Liv. Age 152 :
        245, 738.
    Ophelia.   Blackw. 129 : 66.   Same art. Liv. Age 149 : 33.
    Rosalind.   Blackw. 136 : 399.
    Desdemona.   Blackw. 129 : 324.   Same art. Ecl. M. 96 :
        643.   Liv. Age 149 : 206.   Appleton 25 : 399.
    Portia.   Blackw. 129 : 198.   Same art. Ecl. M. 96 : 478.
        Liv. Age 149 : 145.   Appleton 25 : 312.
    Imogen.   Blackw. 133 : 1.   Same art. Ecl. M. 100 : 299.
    Hermione.   Blackw. 149 : 1.

(**Mathews**, Fanny Aymar.)   A Plea for the Play Writer.
Godey 127: 466 (O. '93).
Woman and Amateur Acting. No. Am. 159: 759 (D. '94).
(**Matthews**, J. B., and J. Brander.)   *See "Matthews, Brander."*
(**Matthews**, J. Brander, and L. Hutton.)   American Actors and
Actresses. Atlan. 59: 421.
(**Matthews**, Brander.) The American on the Stage. Cent. o.
s. 78: 321 (Jl. '79). The Dramatic Author and the
Dramatic Critic. Dr. Mirror 23: 574 (D. 28, '89).
Actors and Actresses of New York. Cent. o. s. 17: 769
(Ap. '79).
A Company of Actors (Comédie Française). Cent. o. s.
16: 837 (O. '78).
Alger's Life of Edwin Forrest. Nation 25: 124.
Dramatic Outlook in America. Harper 78: 924 (My. '89).
Autobiography of Joseph Jefferson. Nation 51: 386.
About the Ballet. Appleton 19: 306.
Sarah Bernhardt. Amer. 1: 92.
Comedies, Light. Cent. o. s. 15: 890.
Comic Dramatist, A French. Atlan. 46: 48.
Modern Comedy. Princ. n. s. 11: 273.
Coquelin. Scrib. 1: 244 (F. '87).
Course of Reading on the Drama. Critic 3: 215.
Damned Plays. Lippinc. 19: 625 (My. '77).
Dramas of Dumas the Elder. Atlan. 48: 383.
Dumas, *fils.* Internat. 10: 503.
Foreign Actors on the American Stage. Cent. o. s. 21:
521 (F. '81).
French Drama in 1820. Amer. 1: 124.
French Plays for American Amateurs. Cent. o. s. 15: 131.
Meilhac and Halévy, Authors of "Frou-Frou." Lippinc.
26: 711 (D. '80).
Molière: The Life and Legend. Lippinc. 23: 431 (Ap. '79).
"The Players." Cent. 21: 28.
Present Tendencies of French Drama. Lippinc. 27: 383
(Ap. '81).
Private Theatricals. Cent. o. s. 15: 430.

Mephistopheles and the Student.   Tait 1: 477.

Mephistopheles, A Night with.   Dub. Univ. 26: 571.

"Merchant of Venice."   (D. J. Snider) J. Spec. Philos. 6:
130, 361.   (R. H. Barham) Bentley 11: 429.   Temp.
Bar 20: 210.   All the Year 43: 495.   Blackw. 40:
429.   (G. Fletcher) Fraser 41: 499, 697.   (J. Spedd-
ing) Cornh. 41: 276.   Same art. Appleton 23: 450.
(A. Lang) Harper 80: 655.   (J. Errington) Month
61: 393.   (W. J. Rolfe) Poet Lore 1: 514.
French Version of.   Lippinc. 35: 78.
Slavonic Parallel to.   (J. G. Fraser) Acad. 27: 330.
Two Legends of.   (G. Chiarini) Chaut. 17: 702 (S. '93).

(Meredith, E. A.)   Talfourd's "Ion."   Canad. Mo. 8: 38.

(Merington, Marguerite.)   Women Characters of Molière.
Chaut. N. '96.   Pub. Opin. 21: 63 (N. 12, '96).

(Merivale, H.)   English Drama of To-day.   Temp. Bar 77:
371.   Same art. Ecl. M. 107: 283.

"Merry Wives of Windsor."   (D. J. Snider) Western 2:
722.   All the Year 47: 77.   (A. Lang) Harper 80: 3.
and Queen Elizabeth.   (A. Morgan) Cath. World 45: 348.

(Mew, J.)   Modern Persian Stage.   Fortn. 65: 902 (Je. '96).

(Meyer, A. N.)   H. Ibsen.   Lippinc. 53: 375 (Mr. '94).

(Meynell, A.)   Sarah Bernhardt.   Art J. 40: 134.

(Michael, H. A.)   Drama in Relation to Truth.   Poet Lore 7:
149 (Mr. '95).

"Midsummer Night's Dream."   Ed. R. 87: 418.   Blackw.
40: 139.   (D. J. Snider) J. Spec. Philos. 8: 165.
All the Year 43: 111.   Fraser 50: 677.   (A. M. Lethe)
Educa. 12: 406 (Mr. '92).   (J. Wedgewood) Contemp.
57: 580.
Daly's Rendering of.   Critic 12: 69.
Fairy Lore in.   (E. G. Skeat) Poet Lore 3: 177.
Revival of.   (G. E. Montgomery) Cosmop. 5: 91.

Millard, Evelyn.   (Mrs. Anthony Hope) The. n. s. 27: 317
(Je. '96).

Modjeska, Helena Benda, Countess Chlapowska, as Juliet. The. '80, 2 : 241.

as Imogen. Critic 12 : 69.

as Lady Macbeth. Critic 15 : 259. Poet Lore 4 : 41 (Ja. '92).

as Portia. Critic 15 : 220.

Chat with. Poet Lore 1 : 524 (N. '89).

in England. (W. Marston) Critic 1 : 144.

(Modjeska, Helena Benda, Countess Chlapowska.) Autobiographic Reminiscences. Arena 1 : 298, 403.

Endowed Theatre and American Stage. Forum 14 : 337 (N. '92).

Success on the Stage. No. Am. 135 : 580 (D. '82).

(Moir, G.) German Criticism of Shakspere. Blackw. 37 : 236, 523, 747; 39 : 699; 40 : 139, 427.

Molière, J. B. P. (A. Lang) Scrib. 9 : 725 (Je. '91). (H. D. Lawhead) Poet Lore (Ap. '96). (J. B. Matthews) Lippinc. 23 : 421 (Ap. '79). (John Coleman) The. n. s. 22 : 128, 184, 315 (S., O., and D. '93). (II. M. Trollope) Fraser 169 : 273. Blackw. 120 : 172. Penny M. 10 : 305. Ecl. M., with portrait, 75 : 372. Tait n. s. 20 : 65, 129. Same art. Ecl. M. 29 : 34. Ed. R. 82 : 172. Same art. Liv. Age 6 : 521. (Sir W. Scott) For. Quar. R. 2 : 306. Same art. Mus. 13 : 113. Mod. R. 109 : 370. (J. B. Matthews) Nation 29 : 129. Mod. R. 145 : 347. St. James' 28 : 97, 188.

and the Doctors of his Day. All the Year 9 : 136. Liv. Age 78 : 448.

and La Grange. Cornh. 41 : 434.

at Home and at the Play. Ev. Sat. 5 : 495.

and Shakspere. (C. Coquelin) Cent. 16 : 819.

and his Satire. (W. Besant) Temp. Bar 33 : 83.

and his Troupe. (W. Besant) Temp. Bar 32 : 374. Liv. Age 110 : 163.

and his Wife. (G. Hogarth) Bentley 4 : 451.

and his World. Temp. Bar 49 : 335. Same art. Liv. Age 133 : 195.

Molière, J. B. P., Career of. Dub. Univ. 71: 345, 470, 553.

Comedies of. (E. I. Sears) Nat. Q. 5: 83.

Début on the Stage. (II. M. Trollope) Blackw. 150: 486.

Funeral of. (P. Kent) The. n. s. 12: 296.

Genius of. Colburn 37: 429.

IIumor of. (A. Tetley) Macmil. 56: 190.

Leaves from the Laurel of. Cornh. 40: 190.

Life and Legend of. (J. B. Matthews) Lippinc. 23: 431.

Life and Times of. Dub. Univ. 66: 3. Same art. Ecl. M. 65: 579.

Life and Writings of. (W. H. Prescott) No. Am. 27: 372.

"Le Misanthrope." (H. M. Trollope) Gent. M. n. s. 40: 192.

"Tartufe." (H. M. Trollope) Blackw. 154: 641 (N. '93).

Maison de, Visit to. Lippinc. 25: 124 (Ja. '80).

Moy Thomas on. Sat. R. 71: 290.

Wife of. (G. Moriarty) Gent. M. n. s. 43: 20.

Woman Characters of. (M. Merington) Chaut. (N. '96). Same art. Pub. Opin. 21: 63 (N. 12, '96).

Recent Edition of Works of. 1875. Ed. R. 142: 337.

Spare Minutes with. (F. R. Thomas) Victoria 31: 118, 306; 32: 36, 438.

(Mollen, J. S.) Freytag on the Technique of the Drama. Dial (Ch.) 18: 77 (F. 1, '95).

(Molloy, J. F.) Kitty Clive. English Illust. 3: 17.

Garrick and his Fellow Players. Eng. Illust. 5: 189.

Nell Gwynn, Player and Courtier. Eng. Illust. 3: 541. Same art. Ecl. M. 107: 263.

(Moncrieff, W. T.) Ellistoniana. Colburn 67: 22, 532; 68: 99, 529; 69: 129, 559.

Monologue, on the French Stage.　Lippinc. 28: 312 (S.
　　'81).

(Monroe, H.)　Hugo on Shakspere.　Dial (Ch.) 7: 181.

Montague, Henry J., and America.　(J. Hatton) The. '78,
　　2: 208.

(Montgomery, G. E.)　Barrett (L.) and His Plays.　Cent. 5:
　　954. (Ap. '84).
　　Dickens on the American Stage.　Amer. 8: 190.
　　"Players'" Club.　Cosmop. 7: 141.
　　Bad Air in the Theatre.　Engin. M. 3: 190 (My.'92).
　　Ideal Dramatic Criticism.　Writer 1: 121.
　　Revival of "Midsummer Night's Dream."　Cosmop. 5:
　　91.

(Montgomery, J. D.)　Macbeth Considered as a Celt.　Na-
　　tional 13: 81.

(Moore, E. A.)　Moral Proportion and Fatalism of Passion in
　　Shakspere.　Poet Lore 7: 75, 551 (Ap. and N. '95).

(Moore, G.)　Dramatic Censorship.　New R. 3: 354.
　　Our Dramatists and their Literature.　Fortn. 52: 620.

(Moore, G. H.)　The First American Theatre.　M. Am. Hist.
　　21: 58.

Moore, Mary.　The. '86, 2: 293, 332.　The. n. s. 26: 5 (Jl.
　　'95).

Moral Influence of the Drama.　(J. M. Buckley, and others)
　　No. Am. 136: 581.

Morality and the Playhouse.　Harper 83: 797 (N. '91).　All
　　the Year 21: 324, 349, 372 (Mr. 6, 13, 20, '69).　Pamph.
　　12: 49.

Morals.　Victoria 25: 739.

Moral Purpose in H. A. Jones's "Dancing Girl."　(J. D.
　　Hunting) The. n. s. 19: 121 (Mr. '92).

Moral Responsibility of Novel and Drama.　Critic 25: 323, 356
　　(N. 17, 24, '94).　*See "Influence," "Church and
　　Drama," etc.*

(**Morehead**, E. D. A.) Dramas of James Dryden Hosken. Acad. 42: 125 (Ag. 13, '92).

(**Morgan**, Appleton.) Hamlet. Cath. World 44: 29.
"Merry Wives" and Queen Elizabeth. Cath. World 45: 348.
Shakspere and his Æsthetic Critics. Cath. World 40: 379.
Shakspere as a Dialect Artist. Cath. World 52: 849.
Shakspere, First Publisher. Cath. World 51: 606.
Shakspere, Text Growth and Vicissitudes of the. Cath. World 46: 68.
Shakspere, Handwriting. Cath. World 50: 165.
Shakspere, How to Study. Cath. World 57: 777.
Shakspere, Much Ado about the Sonnets. Cath. World 42: 212.
Shakspere, "Pericles." Cath. World 50: 723.
Shaksperian Plays, Doubtful. Cath. World 55: 203, 397.
Shaksperian Chronology, A Study in. Cath. World 62: 449.

(**Morgan**, M. H.) Latin Play at Harvard. Harv. Grad. Mo. 2: 345 (Mr. '94).

(**Morley**, G.) Commemorations of Shakspere. Poet Lore 2: 252, 607; 3: 204.
Shaksperian Celebrations. Belgra. 82: 72 (S. '93).

(**Morley**, H.) School for Dramatic Art. The. '80, 1: 76.

(**Morin**, A.) Ventilation of New Paris Theatres. J. Frank. Inst. 76: 369.

(**Morison**, G. S.) Construction of Theatres. Nation 23: 355.

Morris, Clara. (C. Stuart) The. '81, 1: 145.

(**Morris**, Clara.) Reflections of an Actress. No. Am. 153: 329.

Morris, Felix, in "On 'Change." The. '86, 1: 132, 136.

(**Morris**, M.) Hamlet and the Modern Stage. Macmil. 65: 357 (Mr. '92).

(Morrison, G. E.) Past Dramatic Season. The. n. s. 22:
134 (S. 93).

(Morton, E. A.) The Coquelins. The. n. s. 11: 295.

Morton, James Maddison. (W. Goodman) The. '86, 1: 117.

Morton, John Maddison. (C. Scott) Lond. Soc. 49: 66.

(Mosby, E. F.) Hamlet. So. M. 9: 348.
Macbeth. So. M. 9: 348.

Mounting of Plays. Harper 43: 296 (Jl. '71).

Mouth, The Player's. Scrib. 11: 660 (My. '92).

Mowatt, Anna Cora. *See "Mrs. Ritchie."*

"Much Ado About Nothing." (D. J. Snider) Western 2:
641. All the Year 45: 222. (W. J. Rolfe) Poet Lore
4: 184 (Ap. '92). (A. Lang) Harper 83: 489.
Irving's Production of. Sat. R. 63: 875. Knowl. 2:
388, 406. Sat. R. 54: 536. Spec. 55: 1312. (F. Hawkins) The. '82, 2: 212, 294.
(C. A. Wurtzburg) Poet Lore 6: 491 (O. '94); 616
(D. '94).
Character in. (C. A. Wurtzburg) Poet Lore 6: 126. (Mr.
'94).
Dramatic Passion in. (C. A. Wurtzburg) Poet Lore 6:
550 (N. '94).
Introduction to. (C. A. Wurtzburg) Poet Lore 6: 70 (F.
'94).

Munich, Shakspere's Stage at. Poet Lore 1: 47 (Ja. '89).
Theatre in. Temp. Bar 6: 476.

Municipal Theatres. (W. H. Pollock) The. n. s. 25: 15
(Ja. '95).

(Munro, R.) Lady Macbeth. J. Spec. Philos. 21: 30.

(Munsey, Frank A.) Henry Clay Barnabee. Munsey 12:
612 (Mr. '95).

Murdoch, James E. On Acting. Sat. R. 56: 172.
"The Stage." (J. B. Runnion) Dial (Ch.) 1: 107.

(**Murdoch**, J. E.) Short Study of Hamlet. Forum 9: 496 (Jl. '90).

Short Study of Macbeth. Forum 10: 72 (S. '90).

(**Murphy**, B.) F. A. Kemble. " Records of a Girlhood." Cath. World 30: 334.

Murphy, Quarrel of Garrick and. (T. F. Ordish) Bibliog. 6: 37, 65.

Murray, Alma. The. '82. 2: 193, 218.

(**Murray**, H.) The Actor at School. The. n. s. 11: 71.

(**Murray**, J.) Shaksperian Acted Drama. Overland n. s. 22: 355 (O. '93).

(**Murray**, L.) Ophelia. Canad. M. 13: 137.

Music, Incidental, in Plays. (J. A. F. Maitland) The. n. s. 25: 200 (Ap. '95). Blackw. 6: 430. Irish Q. 9: 104. All the Year 26: 369.

How to Write Dramas for. (F. A. Laidlaw) The. n. s. 18: 67.

in Plays. I. Accessorial. II. Incidental. (W. B. Kingston) The. n. s. 25: 143, 290 (Mr., and My. '95).

Music Hall in England, Distinction between, and the Theatre. Spec. 68: 673 (My. 14, '92).

Music Halls. (M. Browne) Argosy 2: 117. (T. Hopkins) Dub. Univ. 92: 192. (G. T. Little) Lond. Soc. 70: 25 (Jl. '96). (D. Wallis) Longm. 22: 163 (Je. '93). Cornh. 60: 68.

Age before. All the Year 31: 175.

Chat about. (H. Louther) Tinsley 27: 364.

Continental. (E. Ballantyne) The. n. s. 17: 121.

London. (P. Fitzgerald) National 15: 379. (F. A. Guthrie) Harper 82: 190 (Ja. '91).

London County Council and. The. n. s. 24: 277 (D. '84).

Morality of. Spec. 63: 461.

Pedigree of. (E. R. Pennell) Contemp. 63: 375 (Ap. '83). Same art. Ecl. M. 120: 792 (Je. '93).

vs. the Drama. Cornh. 15: 119.

17

New York Theatres, Old.   Harper 74: 643 (Mr. '87).
Appleton 8: 576. Atlan. 43: 452; 47: 362.

(Nicholson, B.) "King Edward II." Ath. '87, I: 554.

(Nicholson, C.) "Becket." Month 35: 309.
Guy de Maupassant as a Dramatist. Acad. 39: 265.

(Noel, R. R.) Stage Recollections. Fraser 91: 326.

(Norman, II.) W. Barrett as Hamlet. Nation 39: 396.
Henry Irving in America. Nation 37: 9.

(Northcott, John.) Advantages of Comparison. The. n. s.
26: 83 (Ag. '95).

(Norton, E.) C. Marlowe and his Times. Harv. Mo. I: 50.

Novel and the Drama. Advice to Authors. Blackw. 57: 679.

Novel, Victorian, and Elizabethan Drama. Lippinc. 47: 520
(Ap. '91).

Novels, Dramatization of. (J. B. Matthews) Longm. 14: 588
(O. '89). Ev. Sat. 9: 835.
(J. M. Porter) Macmil. 40: 244.

"Ober Ammergau." *See "Passion Play."*

(Oehlenschlager, A.) Hamlet. Scand. I: 234.

(Ogilvy, R.) Low Life on the Stage. Once a Week 17: 408,
428.

(Ogilvy, Arthur.) Theatricals in Stangate. Once a Week
17: 19 (Jl. 6, '67).

O'Keefe, John. Colburn 16: 345; 17: 17, 564; 47: 232.

(O'Keene, F.) Victorien Sardou at Marley. The. '79, 2:
137.

Old Bowery Theatre. The.   (J. J. McCloskey) Dr. Mirror 37:
939 (Xmas '96).

Old Dry Ink. (Bronson Howard) Dr. Mirror 37: 939
(Xmas, '96).

Oldfield, Anne. Harper 69: 51. (D. Cook) Gent. M. n. s.
28: 157.

Palmer, John, as Joseph Surface. (D. Cook) Gent. M. n. s.
20: 429.

Palmer, Minnie. The. '84, 1: 104.

Panics, Riots, etc. *See "Dangers."*

Pantomime, At a. (F. W. Fairholt) St. James' 3: 193.
and Pandemonium. (G. A. Sala) Belgra. 11: 165.
"Book" of the. (T. E. Pemberton) The. n. s. 27: 25
(Ja. '96).
Decadence of. (C. Dickens, 2nd) The. n. s. 27: 21
(Ja. '96).
English. Chamb. J. 47: 49, 72.
English Origin of. Temp. Bar 55: 93.
Genesis of. (W. J. Lawrence) The. n. s. 25: 28 (Ja.'95).
in United States. (W. J. Lawrence) The. n. s. 27: 83
(F. '96).
Introduction of. Once a Week 26: 77.
Nemesis of. (G. A. Sala) Belgra. 25: 340.
Rehearsals of. Dub. Univ. 38: 39.

Pantomimes. All the Year 17: 189. Temp. Bar 1: 181.
Chamb. J. 41: 30.
Christmas. (T. C. DeLeon) Lippinc. 3: 36.
History of. Fraser 33: 43. Lond. Soc. 7: 204.

Paris, Acting in. Emotional. (K. Venning) The. n. s.
10: 240.
Study of Acting in (Julie M. Everts) Cent. 6: 471 (Jl.
'84). Dub. Univ. 64: 591.
Conservatoire, A Day at the. Lippinc. 20: 512 (O. '77).
Drama before Molière. Cornh. 26: 90.
Drama in. (C. Hervey) Colburn 81: 484; 82: 125, 318.
Dub. Univ. 64: 591. Fraser, 70: 678. Westm. 71:
416.
Drama Since the Revolution. (C. Hervey) Colburn 83:
255, 388.
Playwrights of Paris. (T. Child) Contemp. 51: 712.
Shakspere at the Paris Exposition. (J. C. King) Poet
Lore 1: 560 (D. '89).

Paris, Stage Beauties, Some. (A. Hornblow) Godey 127: 65 (Jl. '93).

 Stage, Favorites of. (A. Hornblow) Munsey 11: 479 591 (Ag. and S. '94).

 Theatre, Mediæval. Cornh. 21: 595.

 Theatres. Harper 8: 311 (F. '54). Harper 35: 239 (Jl. '67). Irish Q. 8: 88. (L. H. Hooper) Appleton 11: 525, 583, 626; 12: 454, 716. (J. B. Runnion) Dial (Ch.) 1: 5. Bentley 25: 369. Blackw. 74: 78. Lond. Soc. 25: 398, 536; 26: 17, 293; 27: 207. House. Words 6: 63. Once a Week. 18: 101, 123. N. Eng. M. 8: 279.

 Theatres and Concerts. (W. F. Apthorp) Scrib. 11: 3, 335, 482, 682 (Ja. '92).

 Theatres, and Molière. Cornh. 26: 90.

 Theatres, Anecdotes of. Bentley 41: 21.

 Theatres, Architecture of. Art J. 31: 265.

 Theatres, Claque in. *See "Applause."*

 Theatres, Foyers of. *See "Foyers."*

 Theatres, in Middle Ages. Cornh. 21: 595.

 Theatres, Scenes from. Dub. Univ. 73: 574. Ev. Sat. 7: 705.

(Parke, F.) Conventionalities of the Drama. Dub. Univ. 83: 503.

(Partridge, W. O.) Drama in Relation to Education. Am. J. Soc. Sci. 21: 188.

(Pascoe, C. E.) First Nights in London Theatres. Amer. 1: 103.

Passion Play of Persia. (G. W. Benjamin) Harper 72: 460 (F. '86).

(Pater, W. H.) "Measure for Measure." Fortn. 22: 652.

(Pater, W.) End of Kings of Shakspere. Scrib. 5: 506.

(Patterson, C. S.) Hamlet. Amer. 5: 185.

(Patterson, Alf.) What to do with Deadheads. The. n. s. 27: 80 (F. '96).

Park Theatre, Old, of New York. Harper 21 : 125(D. '61);
40 : 605 (Mr. '70).

(Parker, Gilbert.) Herbert Beerbohm Tree. Lippinc. 55 :
117 (Ja. '95).

(Parker, Nellie Louise.) Some Neglected Plays. Belgra.
84 : 412 (Ag. '94).
Play Bills, Past and Present. The. n. s. 20 : 8 (Jl. '92).
British Tar on the Stage. The. n. s. 25 : 24 (Ja. 95).

(Parr, J. C. W.) Japanese Theatre. The. '84, 2 : 184.

(Partridge, W. O.) Drama in Relation to Education. Am. J.
Soc. Sci. 21 : 188.

Passion Play (Ober Ammergau). Leisure Hour 20 : 342, 432,
688. The. '80, 1 : 255. Cath. World 12 : 81. Blackw.
107 : 381. Am. Church R. 24 : 187. O. and N. 2 : 173.
Rel. M. 44 : 209. So. M. 11 : 423. Nation 11 : 226. Liv.
Age 27 : 87. (H. Blackburn) Once a Week 23 : 35.
(Mrs. Bushby) Colburn 147 : 288. (R. Ellis) Mo.
Rel. M. 44 : 209. (H. H. Jackson) Cent. 3 : 663,
913 (Mr. and Ap. '83.) (M. D. Conway) Harper 43 :
919 (N. '71).
1860. Macmil. 2 : 463. Same art. Liv. Age 67 : 482.
1870. Harper 42 : 174 (Ja. '71). Month 13 : 340.
1870 and 1880. (W. S. Perry) Ch. R. 35 : 1.
1880. (G. S. Hall) Nation 31 : 110. N. Eng. M. 39 : 794.
Cath. World 31 : 648, 736.
and Symbolic Christianity. (R. St. J. Tyrwhitt) Contemp. 18 : 234.

Passion Play at Brixlegg. All the Year 20 : 397.
in Havana. (B. Peytoulbard) St. James' 46 : 424.
of the Kreuzschule. Lippinc. 17 : 125.
Persian. (M. Arnold) Cornh. 24 : 688. Same art. Liv.
Age 12 : 3. Ecl. M. 78 : 157. Ev. Sat. 12 : 1. Harper
72 : 460.
Tuscan. Sat. R. 56 : 432 (O. 6, '83).

18

Poetry, Dramatic.   Dub. Univ. 23: 19.
  Dramatic English. Quart. 46: 477.   Mod. R. 125: 377.
    Westm. 18: 51.
  Dramatic, English, in Age of Elizabeth.   Brit. Quar. R.
    14: 39.
Polish Theatres.   Sat. R. 73: 385, 507, 737.
(Pollock, Walter Herries.)   Mary Anderson in London.
    Cent. 6: 315 (Je. '84).
  Acting of Garrick as Seen in his own Time. Longm. 6:
    37.
  The Drama.   Contemp. 28: 54.
  False Emphasis.   The. n. s. 26: 85 (Ag. '95).
  "Faust" at the Lyceum.   National 6: 833 (F. '86).
  Hissing in Theatres.   The. n. s. 25: 147 (Mr. '95).
  Irving's "Faust."   Lippinc. 37: 443 (Ap. '86).
  Irving's Stage Management.   Cent. 4: 953 (O. '83).
  Should Shakspere be Acted? National 19: 231 (Ap. '92).
  Shaksperian Criticism.   19th Cent. 11: 915 (Je. '82).
  A Glance at the Stage.   National 5: 646 (Jl. '85).
  Stage Swordsmanship.   The. n. s. 27: 321 (Je. '96).

(Pollock, J.) For and Against the Drama. 19th Cent. 1: 611.
  German and French Drama.   Contemp. 21: 335.
  Dramatic Art.   Contemp. 23: 363.
  French Drama.   Contemp. 21: 335.
  French Comedy.   Contemp. 18: 43.
  German Drama.   Contemp. 21: 335.

(Pollock, F., and W. H.) French Drama in London.   Dark
    Blue 2: 102.

(Poole, J.) Theatre Royal, Little Pedlington. Colburn 49:
    101, 557.

(Porter, Charlotte.)· Richard Mansfield as Richard III.   Poet
    Lore 2: 30 (Ja. '90).
  Open Letter to Ada Rehan.   Poet Lore 2: 291 (N. '90).
  Browning's Tribute to Shakspere.   Poet Lore 3: 216.

(Porter, J. M.) Dramatization of Novels.   Macmil. 40: 244.

"**Promise** of May." *See " Tennyson, Alfred."*

Pronunciation, an Epidemic of Slovenliness in. (G. W
Dancy) The. n. s. 20 : 97 (S. '92).

(**Prothero,** G. W.) A Greek Play at Cambridge. Cent. 6 :
411 (Je. '84).

Proverbes Dramatiques. (T. Le Clercq) Lon. M. 12 : 17.

Provinces, Criticism in the. The. n. s. 28 : 143 (S. '96).

Provincial Playhouse, in a. (A. Price) Lond. Soc. 56 : 524.

Public, the Actor, the Manager and the. (John Malone)
Forum 20 : 235 (O. '95).
and the Stage. (Edw. Fuller) Lippinc. 46 : 564 (O. '90).
as Fetish. (A. B. Walkley) The. n. s. 24 : 283 (D. '94).
What does the, want ? (W. Archer) The. '85, 1 : 269.

Public's Point of View, The. (Chas. Dickens 2d) The. n. s.
24 : 220 (N. '94).

"**Pudd'nhead** Wilson." *See " Frank Mayo."*

Puritan on Plays. (G. M. Fenn) The. n. s. 25 : 73.

Puritans and the Theatre. Cong. 1 : 592.
Opposition to the Drama. No. Brit. 25 : 1.
and Actors. (W. Wheater) Gent. M. n. s. 50 : 178 (F.
'93).

"**Pygmalion** and Galatea," Mary Anderson in. *See " Mary
Anderson."*

(**Pyne,** J.) Comic Drama of the Restoration. National Q.
34 : 306.

(**Quilter,** H.) Decline of the Drama. Contemp. 51 : 547.
Same art. Ecl. M. 108 : 824.

(**Quincy,** J. P.) A Difficulty in " Hamlet." Atlan. 49 : 388.

Rachel, Eliza Felix. Harper 8: 133 (D. '53); 10: 129,
414 (D. '54, F. '55); 11: 12, 559, 842 (Je., S. and
N. '55); 12: 852 (My. '56); 16: 703 (Ap. '58); 17:
129 (Je. '58); 33: 528 (S. '66). Blackw. 132: 271.
Same art. Ecl. M. 97: 587, Liv. Age 155: 156. Belgra.
34: 154. Bentley 43: 140; 45: 530. Cornh. 9: 440;
Liv. Age 56: 755; 58: 297; 67: 6. Putnam 6: 290.
Sharpe 27: 87. Galaxy 2: 84. (D. Cook) Gent. M.
n. s. 25: 188. (Mme. de Marguerites) Sharpe 15: 13.
(Mrs. A. (W. H.) Kennard) 19th Cent. 14: 1030 (D.
'83). (H. S. Wilson) Lond. Soc. 25: 222.

and Sarah Bernhardt. (J. P. Simpson) The. '80, 2: 23.

and Charlotte Cushman. (Mme. de Marguerites) Sharpe
15: 13.

My Acquaintance with. (C. Marie) Harper 16: 805 (My.
'58).

Death of. (R. Davey) The. '80, 1: 273.

in United States. The. '82, 2: 200.

Letters of. The. '83, 1: 342.

Teacher of. M. Samson. (Lucy H. Hooper) Lippinc.
29: 617 (Je. '92).

Racine and his Tragedies. Dub. Univ. 74: 225. Ev. Sat.
8: 341.

(Ramsay, J.) Irving and Diderot's " Paradoxe." National 3:
99 (Mr. '84).

(Randolph, H. F.) London Theatres 1550–1650. N. Eng.
M. n. s. 10: 318 (My. '94).

Rankin, Arthur McKee. Colburn 167: 302.

Raymond, John T., as Colonel Sellers. (W. D. Howells)
Atlan. 35: 749.

(Reade, A. B.) Cheap Theatres and the Lord Chamberlain.
Peop. J. 3: 97.

Reade, Charles. Personal Reminiscences of. (J. Coleman)
Lippinc. 34: 146, 234, 354 (Ag., S. and O. '84).

(Reade, Chas.) Drama of " Drink." Spec. 55: 1079.

19

(**Reade,** W. B.)　English Stage.　Galaxy 3 : 271.

Reader of Plays.　(D. Cook) Belgra. 36 : 432.

Realism.　(P. Beck) The. '83, 2 : 127.　(W. Gordon) The.
　　'80, 2 : 283.
　　in Modern Drama.　(H. D. Traill) 19th Cent. 26 : 864
　　　(D. '94).
　　in Plays and Playing.　(G. S. Power) Colburn 169 : 10.

Realism, Stage : Is it Outdone?　(A. W. a Beckett) The.
　　n. s. 28 : 132 (S. '96).

Realist, Dramatic, to his Critics.　(G. B. Shaw) New R. 11 :
　　56 (Jl. '94).　Same art. Ecl. M. 123 : 326.

Recitation, Dramatic.　(F. E. M. Steel) Westm. 132 : 530.

Recollections, My Earliest Stage.　(Chas. W. Couldock)
　　Dr. Mirror 35 : 886 (Xmas, '95).

Reform, Dramatic.　(T. J. Serle) Colburn 166 : 8.　Victoria
　　31 : 1.

(**Reed,** J. P.)　Beauties on the American Stage.　Cosmop. 14 :
　　294 (Ja. '93).

Reed, Alf. German.　(M. Watson) The. n. s. 25 : 221 (Ap.
　　'95).

Rehan, Ada.　(C. Porter) Poet Lore 2 : 591 (N. '90).

Religion, the Bible, and the Stage.　Spec. 70 : 155 (F. 4, '93).

Religion of the Stage.　The. n. s. 26 : 313 (D. '95).　(C.
　　Lamb) Colburn 6 : 405.　*See " Church and Drama,"*
　　" Morality," etc.

Reminiscences, Theatrical.　All the Year 64 : 32.

Reminiscences.　*See " Memories and Reminiscences," etc.*

Renaissance of the Drama.　*See " H. A. Jones," " Revolu-*
　　tion," etc.

Restoration, Comic Dramatists of the.　(T. B. Macaulay)
　　Ed. R. 72 : 49.　(J. Pyne) Nat. Q. 34 : 306.

Review of Pollock's Reminiscences of Macready.　Sat. R.
　　58 : 730.

Revolution, Theatrical. The. n. s. 22: 189, 254, 324 (O., N. and D. '93); 23: 83, 137, 191, 265, 306 (F., Mr., Ap., My. and Je. '94); 24: 19 (Jl. '94).

(Reynolds, J. H.) John Philip Kemble. So. Lit. Mess. 19: 164.

(Rhodes, A.) French Plays. Galaxy 20: 372.
French Theatre. Galaxy 19: 22.
V. Sardou. Galaxy 17: 485.
French Theatre. Galaxy 19: 22.

(Richardson, L.) James Lewis. Metrop. 4: 341 (D. '96).

Richelieu, (Cardinal), Armand Jean du Plessis, as a Dramatist. (L. H. Hooper) Lippinc. 23: 627.

"Richelieu." *See "Lord Lytton."*

Righton, Edw. The. n. s. 26: 102 (Ag. '95).

(Righton, Edw.) "The Happy Land," a Suppressed Burlesque. The. n. s. 28: 63 (Ag. '96).

Rip Van Winkle, Legend of. Harper 67: 617.
Original of. Lon. M. 5: 229.
See also "Joseph Jefferson," etc.

Ristori, Adelaide. Harper 11: 416, 559 (Ag. and O. '55); 33: 528 (S. '66); 34: 123 (D. '66). (K. Field) Atlan. 19: 493. Cornh. 8: 172. (K. Field) Harper 34: 740. Putnam 10: 363.
Acting of. (O. B. Frothingham) Nation 2: 254, 336.
as Marie Antionette. (K. Field) Lippinc. 1: 175 (F. '68).

Ritchie, Mrs. Anna Cora Mowatt. (M. Howitt) Howitt 3: 146, 167, 181.
Autobiography of. (Dr. Walker) Evang. R. 8: 564.
Liv. Age 41: 33.

(Ritchie, Mrs.) Frances Anne Kemble. Macmil. 68: 190 (Jl. '93).

(Robbins, A. W.) Dramatic Expression. Lippinc. 53: 242 (F. '94).

(**Robertson**, D.) Australian Drama. The. n. s. 9: 23.

Robertson, T. W., the Younger. (A. Escott) The. n. s. 26: 29 (Jl. '95).

Robertson, Johnstone Forbes. The. '83, 1: 311. The. n. s. 23: 8 (Ja. '94). The. n. s. 27: 5 (Ja. '96).

(**Robertson**, Johnstone Forbes.) Helena Modjeska. St. James' 48: 16.

(**Robertson**, J. G.) Twenty-five Years of a German Court Theatre. National 25: 247 (Ap. '95).

Reminiscences, Autobiographical, Modjeska, Helena Benda, Countess Chlapowska. Arena 1: 298, 403.

Robertson, Mary Lytton. The. '80, 1: 255.

Robertson, T. W. Lippinc. 15: 768 (Je. '75). (W. W. Jones) The. '79, 1: 355. (F. Hawkins) Acad. 43: 488 (Je. 3, '93). Temp. Bar. 44: 199. Ev. Sat. 10: 270. Lond. Soc. 42 (D. '82).
Comedies of. Broadw. 6: 570. O. and N. 3: 617. Ev. Sat. 9: 339.
Death of. Ev. Sat. 10: 186.
Pemberton's Life of. Spec. 70: 192 (F. 11, '93).
"School." Once a Week 20: 238.

(**Robins**, Elizabeth.) Across America with Edwin Booth. Univ. R. 7: 375 (Jl. '90).
Stage Buffoons. Atlan. 51: 529.

(**Robinson**, P.) "Titus Andronicus." Contemp. 65: 392 (Mr. '94). Same. art. Ecl. M. 122: 547 (Ap. '94).

(**Robinson**, L.) Natural History of the Hiss. No. Am. 157: 104 (Jl. '93).

Robinson, Mary, as Perdita. (D. Cook) Once a Week 12: 625, 648. Temp. Bar 51: 536.

Robinson, Fred'k. (D. Cook) Gent. M. n. s. 28: 715. (G. A. Sala) Atlan. 13: 715 (W. J. Prowse) Sharpe 35: 192.

(**Robb**, T. D.) Elizabethan Drama and the Victorian Novel. Lippinc. 47: 520 (Ap. '91).

(**Rodgers, E. B.**) Japanese Theatre. Outing 25: 191 (D.
    '94).

(**Rogers, F.**) Marlowe's "Tamburlane the Great." Acad.
    34: 244.

Rome, Theatre of. Colburn, 47: 31.

(**Rolfe, W. J.**) Division of Plays of Shakspere into Scenes.
    Lit. World (Bost.) 13: 11.

    Eyes of Shakspere. Poet Lore 1: 479.

    "Much Ado About Nothing." Poet Lore 4: 184 (Ap.
        '92).

    "Julius Cæsar." Poet Lore 6: 7 (Ja. '94).

    "Merchant of Venice." Poet Lore 3: 514.

    "Tempest." Poet Lore 3: 190.

Romeo, Study of. (J. J. Chapman) Atlan. 78: 707 (N. '96).
    and Rosaline. (L. M. Griffiths) Poet Lore 1: 205.

"**Romeo** and Juliet." (D. J. Snider) Western 1: 37, 71. All
    the Year 44: 42. Temp. Bar. 9: 209. Blackw. 37:
    523. Same art. Mus. 26: 615.

    Act. 3, Scene 2. (W. W. Lloyd) Ath. '84, 2: 402. (A.
    Williams and others) Ath. '84, 2: 465.

    At the Lyceum. (E. K. Russell) Macmil. 46: 325.

    Characters of Peter and the Apothecary. Cornh. 49: 188.

    Corte's Account of. Antiq. n. s. 3: 265. (F. O'Kane)
    The. n. s. 26: 149 (S. '95).

    Criticism and Acting of. Westm. 44: 1.

    in French. (C. Seymour) Poet Lore 3: 27.

    Irving in. *See "Irving."*

    Local Color in. (W. Archer) Gent. M. n. s. 33: 440.
    Same art. Ecl. M. 104: 67.

    Myths of. (W. Archer) National 4: 441 (D. '84).

    Story of. (H. B. Wheatley) Antiq. n. s. 5: 250; 6: 246.

    Text of. (F. G. Fleay) Macmil. 36: 195. All the
    Year 49: 157.

    See "Juliet," "Shakspere," etc. The. '83, 2: 1.

Romeos, Ancient and Modern. (S. J. Hart) The. '82, 1:
    148.

Rorke, Kate.   The. n. s. 22: 16 (Jl. '93); 24: 157 (O. '94).

Rorke, Mary.   The. '82, 2: 1, 60; '84, 2: 109, 162.
in "Harbor Lights." The. '86, 1: 117, 162.

Rosalind, Shakspere's Character of.   Cornh. 16: 474.
(Lady Martin) Blackw. 136: 399.   The. '85, 1: 127.
a Few Words about Miss Faucit's.   Poet Lore 1: 145
(Mr.'89).
on the Stage.   (R. G. White) Atlan. 51: 248.
Miss Faucit as.   *See "Miss Faucit."*
Mrs. Langtry as.   *See "Mrs. Langtry."*
Julia Marlowe as.   *See "Julia Marlowe Taber."*
Mrs. Siddons as.   *See "Mrs. Siddons."*
See "Shakspere," "As You Like It," etc.

(Roscoe, E.)   Hamlet and the Critics.   Victoria 20: 502.
Hamlet, Gervinus' Criticism on.   Victoria 21 : 338.
Ophelia.   Victoria 18: 117.

(Rose, Edw.)   Comédie Française.   The. '79, 1 : 311.
Kissing on the Stage.   The. n. s. 25: 149 (Mr.'95).
Shakspere and History.   Fraser 93 : 546.
Shakspere as an Adapter.   Macmil. 39 : 69.
Wagner as a Dramatist.   Fraser 99: 519.

Rose, Edw. and Anthony Hope.   "Prisoner of Zenda." (L. B.
Ellis) Illust. (Je. and Jl.'96).

Roselle, Amy.   The. '78, 2 : 336.   The. '84, 1 : 152.

(Rosenfeld, Sidney.)   Playwriting.   Author 3 : 142.

(Ross, Morris.)   Deterioration of the Stage.   Poet Lore 3 :
353 (Jl. '91).

Rossi, Ernesto, and St. Petersburg.   (A. Monroe) The. n. s.
26: 24 (Jl.'95).
as Hamlet.   (W. B. Kingston) The. '84, 1 : 173; 2:
90.

Ryan, Katic. The. '81, 1 : 103.

Ryder, John, Recollections of. (H. Turner) The. '85, 1 : 222.

St. John, Florence. The. n. s. 22 : 252 (N. '93).

(St. Maur, Harry.) Jane Hading. Munsey 14 : 159 (N. '95).

(Sage, A.) Hamlet of the Stage. Atlan. 23 : 665; 24 : 188.

(Saintsbury, G.) French Tragedy. Fraser 100 : 456.

(Sala, G. A.) Stage Costumes. Belgra. 8 : 101.

> Comedies of William Cobbett. Belgra 25 : 465. (Fred'k Robson) Atlan. 13 : 715.
>
> Pantomime and Pandemonium. Belgra. 11 : 165.
>
> Nemesis of Pantomime. Belgra. 25 : 340.

Salaries, Actors and their. Harper 2 : 403 (F. '51) (A. à Becket) The. n. s. 25 : 209 (O. '95).

(Salmon, Edw.) Democracy and the Drama. National 12 : 398 (N. '88).

Salvini, Alexander. (M. Aldrich) Arena 7 : 129 (Ja. '93).

Salvini, Tommaso. Sat. R. 57 : 345, 373, 474. Temp. Bar 57 : 67. Spec. 57 : 376. St. James' 36 : 329. (H. B. Bedford) Month 27 : 288. (H. James, Jr.) Atlan. 51 : 377. (E. Lazarus) Cent. 1 : 110 (N. '81). (W. E. Henley) National 3 : 199 (Ap. '84). Same art. Liv. Age 161 : 468. (W. R. Balch). Amer. 1 : 141.

> and Mr. Irving. Gent. M. n. s. 14 : 609.
>
> as Hamlet. Gent. M. n. s. 15 : 46.
>
> as King Lear. Cent. 5 : 563 (F. '84). The. n. s. 20 : 281 (D. '92). (E. Lazarus) Cent. 4 : 88 (My. '83).
>
> as Othello. Lippinc. 12 : 742 (D. '73). (J. H. Browne) Galaxy 16 : 819. (R. G. White) Nation 17 : 46. (F. Kemble) Temp. Bar 71 : 368.
>
> as Saul in Alfieri's tragedy. (E. Shinn) Nation 19 : 14.
>
> Autobiography of. (J. B. Runnion) Dial (Ch.) 15 : 298 (N. 16, '93).
>
> On Shakspere. (H. Zimmern) Gent. M. n. s. 32 : 131.

(**Salvini**, Tommaso.) Some Views of Acting. Cent. 19 : 194.

Impressions of Some of Shakspere's Characters. Cent. 1 : 117 (N. '81).

Impressions of Lear. Cent. 5 : 563 (F. '84).

Leaves from the Autobiography of. Cent. 23 : 230 (D. '92) ; 45 : 588 (F. '83) ; 46 : 90, 927 (My., and O. '93).

(**Samson**, Adelaide Louise.) Seven Notable American Stars. Metrop. 4 : 366 (D. '96).

Samson, M., Teacher of Rachel. (L. H. Hooper) Lippinc. 29 : 617 (Ja. '82).

(**Sarcey**, Francisque.) At Chicago. Scrib. 13 : 677 (My. '93).

French Comedy. 19th Cent. 6 : 182.

Sardou, Victorien. Harper 47 : 841. (J. B. Matthews) Internat. R. 7 : 552. (P. Féval) Ev. Sat. 1 : 719. (A. W. Howard) Munsey 12 : 137 (D. '94). (P. Black) Lippinc. 10 : 314.

at Marley. (F. O'Kane) The. '79, 2 : 137.

Breakfast with. (A. Rhodes) Galaxy 17 : 485.

"Cléopatra." (C. Seymour) Poet Lore 2 : 654 (D. '90). Art J. 44 : 98 (Jl. '92).

"Daniel Rochat." The. '80, 1 : 154.

"Fédora." (W. F. Waller) The. '83, 1 : 85, 362, 378.

"Georgette." (A. Langel) Nation 42 : 9.

"Madame Sans Gêne." (A. Langel) Nation 57 : 445 (D. 14, '93).

"Théodora." (A. Langel) Nation 42 : 9. (J. Bryce) Contemp. 47 : 266 (F. '85). Same art. Liv. Age 164 : 733 (Mr. '85).

"Thermidor." Sat. R. 73 : 626. (A. Goldemar) Fortn. 57 : 770 (Ja. '92).

(**Sargent**, Franklin H.) Shall We Have an American Conservatoire? Cent. 6 : 475 (Jl. '84).

Dramatic Teaching Abroad. Looker On 1 : 522 (Mr. '96).

20

(Sargent, W.)   The French Drama.   No. Am. 78 : 319.

Scenery, Dress, and Decorations.   (G. Turner) The. '80, 1 :
      350.

Schiller.   Dramatic Character of.   So. Lit. J. 4 : 70, 327.
      Shakspere, and Æschylus.   Blackw. 69 : 641.
      "Maria Stuart."   (H. S. Wilson) The. '80, 2 : 167.

Schlegel's Lectures on the Drama.   Portf. (Den.) 17 : 477.
      on the Drama.   (W. Hazlitt) Ed. R. 26 : 67.

(Schleuther, Paul.)   Eleanora Duse.   Looker On (Mr. '96).

School of Dramatic Art.   Spec. 66 : 169.   (H. Aïdé) 19th
      Cent. 11 : 567 (Ap. '82).   (F. C. Burnand) 19th Cent.
      11 : 753 (My. '82).   (C. Scott) The. '82, 2 : 193.
      (H. Aïdé) The. '82, 1 : 73.   (H. Morley) The. '80, 1 :
      76.   (S. J. A. Fitz-Gerald) The. n. s. 25 : 344 (Je. '95).
      The New.   (A. W. Pinero) The. n. s. 13 : 317.
      London as.   Sat. R. 66 : 522 (N. 3, '88).
      Possibilities of a.   Sat. R. 66 : 581 and 615 (N. 17 and 24,
      '88).
      Provinces as a.   Sat. R. 66 : 433 (O. 13, '88).
      Dramatic Teaching Abroad.   (F. H. Sargent) Looker
      On 1 : 522 (Mr. '96).

"School for Scandal."   *See "R. B. Sheridan," etc.*

(Schovelin, T. A.)   Henrik Ibsen.   Scand. 1 : 11, 133.

(Schuyler, E.)   Myths of "Hamlet."   Nation 10 : 170.

(Schwab, Fred'k A.)   New York Season, '93 and '94.   Cos-
      mop. 17 : 18 (My. '94).

Scotland, Drama in.   Hogg 8 : 392, 412.

Scott, Clement.   The. '86, 1 : 1.

(Scott, Clement.)   A Critic of the Critics Criticized.   The. n. s.
      13 : 297.
      A School of Dramatic Art.   The. '82, 2 : 193.
      First Night Criticism.   The. n. s. 24 : 100 (S. '94).
      Criticism in Advance.   The. n. s. 24 : 158 (O. '94).
      "Hamlet."   The. '84, 2 : 243.

(**Scott,** Clement.) James Maddison Morton. Lond. Soc. 49: 66.
  The Modern Society Play. The. n. s. 25: 6 (Ja. '95).
  The New Dictator. The. n. s. 25: 263 (My. '95).
  Two Dramatic Revolutions. No. Am. 157: 476 (O. '93).
  Why Do We Go to the Play? The. n. s. 11: 117.
  Worship of Bad Plays. The. n. s. 16: 261.

(**Scott,** Sir Walter.) Braden's Life of John P. Kemble. Quart.
  34: 197.
  Life and Writings of Molière. For. Quar. R. 2: 306.
  Same art. Mus. 13: 113.

Scribe, Augustin Eugène. Harper 22: 849. (J. D. Os-
  borne) Scrib. 17: 59 (N. '78). (J. P. Simpson) The.
  '80, 2: 333.
  "Adrienne Lecouvreur." (C. E. Meetkerke) Argosy 55:
  106 (F. '93). Temp. Bar 49: 534. Appleton's 24: 250.

(**Scudamore,** E. R.) Japanese Theatre. Cosmop. 10:
  685.

(**Sears,** E. I.) Modern French Drama. National Q. 1: 64.

"**Second** Mrs. Tanqueray, The." *See "A. W. Pinero."*

(**Sedgwick,** A. G.) A School for Actors. Nation 39: 195.
  Jefferson as Rip Van Winkle. Nation 9: 247.
  Lyceum School for Actors. Nation 39: 195.

Sensation Scenes. (W. J. Lawrence.) Gent. M. n. s. 37:
  400.

(**Serle,** T. J.) Dramatic Reform. Colburn 166: 8.

(**Seton,** M.) "Hamlet" and "Macbeth" at the Lyceum. Colburn 160: 175.
  Recent Shaksperian Revivals. Colburn 160: 175, 346.

(**Severance,** Alice.) Julia Marlowe Taber. Godey 132: 401
  (Ap. '96).

(**Seymour,** Chas.) "Hamlet" at the Comédie Française.
  Poet Lore 1: 571 (D. '89).
  "Romeo and Juliet" in French. Poet Lore 3: 27.
  Sardou's "Cléopatra." Poet Lore 2: 654 (D. '90).

Shakspere, William.   Ath. '89, 2 : 139.   Spec. 62 : 517.   (C. W. Franklyn) Westm. 132 : 348.   Belgra. 78 : 398 (Ag. '92).   (J. Stoughton) Leisure Hour 13 : 215, 279. No. Brit. 12 : 115.   Retros. 7 : 378.   Westm. 20 : 151; 26 : 30.   Fraser 21 : 493, 740.   (Cardinal Wiseman) Cath. World 1 : 548.   (A. King) Argosy 16 : 216.   Lond. Quart. R. 22 : 201.   (M. Bell) Cath. World 29 : 67. Canad. M. 17 : 408.   Wes. J. 6 : 273, 545.   Lond. Soc. 5 : 413.

> NOTE.— For *Plays, Characters,* and *Actors,* see the several names of same.

A French View of.   (Ernest Brain) The. n. s. 27 : 208 (Ap. '96).

Actors, Original, of his Plays.   Temp. Bar 53 : 252.

An Actor's Notes on.   (H. Irving) 19th. Cent. 5 : 260.

an American Point of View, from.   (J. G. Shea) Cath. World 25 : 422.

and his Æsthetic Critics.   (A. Morgan) Cath. World 40 : 379.

and his Critics.   So. Lit. Mess. 4 : 132.   Knick. 32 : 518.   Hogg 14 : 345.   Dub. Univ. 61 : 3.

and the Church.   (John Malone) The Seminary 1 : 8, 9, 11 (Jl. '93).

and the Drama.   Blackw. 59 : 534.

and Gloucestershire.   (W. P. Fillimore) Antiq. n. s. 4 : 10.

and History.   Knowl. 11 : 75.   (E. Rose) Macmil. 39 : 69.

and Holinshed.   (W. C. Pell) Harper 23 : 486 (S. '61).

and Ben Jonson, Quarrel Between.   No. Brit. 52 : 394.

and the Jews.   (J. N. Hales) Eng. Hist. R. 9 : 652 (O. '94).

and John Lyly.   (H. Davis) Poet Lore 5 : 177 (Ap. '93).

Shakspere, William, Villains of. St. James' 27: 632.
>What Lurks Behind. (W. Whitman) Critic 4: 145.
>Why Did He Write Tragedies? Cornh. 42: 153.
>Wisdom of Life. (E. Dowden) Fortn. 50: 405.
>Without End. (H. S. Wilson) Gent. M. n. s. 41: 428.
>Women of. (E. Dowden) Contemp. 47: 517. Same art. Liv. Age 165: 405.
>Worship of. (O. B. Frothingham) Cent. 7: 780.
>Young Men of. Westm. 106: 452.

Shaksperian Chronology. (Appleton Morgan) Cath. World 62: 449.
>Acted Drama. (J. Murray) Overland n. s. 22: 355 (O. '93).
>Festival, 1864. Chamb. J. 41: 337. (D. Cook) Once a Week 10: 104.
>Jubilee and Festivals. Chamb. J. 41: 123.
>Jubilee of 1769. Broadw. 3: 317. Dub. Univ. 65: 603.
>Meeting at "Garrick's Head." Lon. M. 18: 9.
>Plays, Doubtful. (Appleton Morgan) Cath. World 55: 203, 397.
>Revivals, Garrick and. Temp. Bar 86: 496.
>Revivals in London. (J. R. Sturgis) Internat. R. 6: 650.
>Revivals, Recent. (M. Seton) Colburn 160: 175, 346.

(Sharp, R. F.) Pinero (A. W.) and Farce. The. n. s. 20: 154 (O. '92).

(Sharp, W.) Maurice Maeterlinck. Acad. 41: 270 (Mr. 19, '92).

"Shaughraun." *See "Boucicault."*

(Shaw, George Bernard.) A Dramatic Realist to his Critics. New R. 11: 56 (Je. '94). Same art. Ecl. M. 123: 326.
>Bernhardt and Duse in "Magda." Sat. R. 79: 787 (Je. 15, '95). The Old Acting and the New. Sat. R. (D. 14, '95).

(Shea, Thos. E.) Glance at Lawrence Barrett. Donahue (S. '96).

Sheridan, Richard Brinsley. Harper 8: 215; 26: 72; 60: 505. (A. V. Dicey) Nation 39: 136. The. n. s. 27: 332 (Je. '96).

Mrs. Oliphant's Life of. *See "Mrs. Oliphant," etc.*

and his Biographers. (J. B. Matthews) Princ. n. s. 13: 292.

as a Dramatist. (J. B. Matthews) Amer. 1: 205, 221.

"Critic." (J. B. Matthews) Lippinc. 24: 629 (N. '79).

"Rivals." Foster Mo. Ref. 1: 15.

"Rivals" and "School for Scandal." All the Year 58: 541, 557.

"Rivals" and "School for Scandal," Original Cast of. (A. Brereton) The. '84, 1: 171.

"School for Scandal." (F. Wedmore) Acad. 21: 109. (P. Fitzgerald) The. '82, 1: 171. (A. G. Whitian) Atlan. 52: 566.

"School for Scandal" at Boston Museum. (H. James, Jr.) Atlan. 34: 754.

(Sherwood, M. E. W.) Recollections of Actresses. Lippinc. 53: 92 (Ja. '94).

(Shinn, E.) T. Salvini. Nation 19: 14.

(Shuttleworth, H. C., N. Hall and). Duty of Church as to the Theatre. Chr. Lit. 11: 302 (S. '94).

Shylock. (M. Jostrow) Penn Mo. 11: 725 (M. D. Conway) 19th Cent. 7: 828. (T. Martin) The. '79, 2: 253.

in Germany. (W. B. Kingston) The. '80, 1: 17, 86.

Original of. (S. R. Lee) Gent. M. n. s. 24: 185.

v. Antonio. (C. Edwards) Contin. M. 3: 539. (C. H. Phelps) Atlan. 57: 463.

Whitewashed. Temp. Bar 45: 65. Same art. Ecl. M. 85: 617.

Siberia, Theatres in. Harper 37: 457 (S. '68).

Siam, Theatre in Bankok. Harper 41: 362 (Ag. '70).

(**Sichel,** Walter S.) The Stage "Faust." National 6: 211
(O. '85).

(**Siddons,** J. H.) British Stage of 19th Century. Foster
Mo. Ref. 18: 565, 639; 19: 14, 139, 245.
Sarah Kemble Siddons. Harper 26: 790 (My. '63).
Theatrical Recollections. Temp. Bar 56: 458.

Siddons, Mrs. Scott. Victoria 9: 60.

Siddons, Sarah Kemble. Harper 26: 72.
(S. S. Conant) Harper 44: 184 (Ja. '72).
(F. A. Kemble) Harper 28: 364 (F. '64).
(J. H. Siddons) Harper 26: 790 (My. '63).
as Rosalind. Poet Lore 1: 196 (Ap. '89).

(**Sigmund,** G. F.) Theatres 2000 Years Ago. Luth. Q. 3:
124.

Sixteenth Century, Drama of. *See "Early Drama."*

(**Simons,** L.) Ibsen as an Artist. Westm. 140: 506 (N. '93).

(**Simpson,** J. P.) The Claque. The. '79, 1: 160.
Rachel and Sarah Bernhardt. The. '80, 2: 23.
Eugène Scribe. The. '80, 2: 333.
Benjamin Webster. The. '82, 2: 83.

(**Skeat,** E. G.) Fairy Lore in "Midsummer Night's Dream."
Poet Lore 3: 177.

(**Slater,** J. W.) Imitation or Mimicry. J. Sci. 21: 475.

(**Slade,** R. Jope.) Playgoers' Club. The. n. s. 22: 273 (N.
'93).

(**Smith,** M. E.) Actors in England in Olden Days. Tinsley
34: 619.

(**Smith,** L.) Is Courtesy Extinct Among the Audiences? The.
n. s. 14: 10 (Jl. '89).

Smith, Wm., 1730-1819. The Original Charles Surface.
(D. Cook) Gent. M. n. s. 19: 261.
Recollections of. Colburn 51: 323.

(**Spielhagen**, F.)   Modern German Drama and its Authors.
Cosmop. 17: 177 (Je. '94).

(**Spink**, Wm.)   Shakspere as a Dramatic Model.   National 6:
384 (Nov. '85).   Same art. Ecl. M. 106: 86.

(**Spofford**, A. R.)   The French Drama.   No. Am. 81: 336.

Stage, English.   National 2: 412.   (T. Taylor) Ev. Sat. 7:
193.   Westm. 59: 89.   (W. B. Reade) Galaxy 3: 271.
Dark Blue 2: 635.

and the Poet.   (Lady Pollock) Temp. Bar 44: 331.

Anecdotes of.   Ecl. M. 26: 178.

Annals of.   Mod. R. 125: 337.

Anomalies.   (H. S. Edwards) Macmil. 41: 322.   Same
art. Appleton 23: 358.

Appointments.   All the Year 10: 229.

Arrangements in Theaters.   Appleton 3: 589.

Art To-Day.   The. n. s. 24: 151 (O. '94).

as a Trade.   Sat. R. 76: 678 (D. 16, '93).

As it Was.   (H. W. Frost) Galaxy 16: 483, 599.

As it Was in 1850.   Bentley 27: 298.

Banquets.   Ev. Sat. 12 : 153.

Bunn on the.   Mod. R. 152: 459.

Chronicles of the.   (P. Fitzgerald) Month 43 : 81, 507; 42 :
71, 535.

Costumes.   (G. A. Sala) Belgra. 8: 101.

Door Lover, A.   The. n. s. 19: 245 (My '92).

Door, Through the.   The. n. s. 25: 63 (F. '95).

Doors.   All the Year 37: 85.

Dresses of 18th Cent.   Chamb. J. 69: 789 (D. '92).

Emotion.   Bentley 51 : 45.

English, Annals of.   Chamb. J. 41 : 317.

English, Early.   (J. L. Stewart) Canad. Mo. 14: 33.
Temp. Bar 53: 243.

English, Grand Days of the. (Olive Logan) Harper 59 : 48.

English, in Time of Charles II.   Temp. Bar 53: 554.

English, Present State of (1871). Temp. Bar 33: 456.

English, Present State of the (1874).   Temp. Bar 40, 470.

(**Stephens,** H. B.) Modern Theatres and Intellectuality. Canad. Mo. 17: 368.

(**Stevens,** G. W.) The New Henrik Ibsen. New R. 12: 39 (Ja. '95). Same art. Liv. Age 205: 239 (Ap. 27, '95).

(**Stevenson,** E. I.) College Theatricals. No. Am. 158: 510 (Ap. '94).

Stevenson, Robert Louis, as a Dramatist. (L. Johnson) Acad. 43: 473 (Je. 3, '93).

(**Stewart,** J. L.) Early English Stage. Canad. Mo. 14: 33.

Stirling, Mrs. (Fanny Clifton). The. '83, 1: 385. (Arthur Escott) The. n. s. 27: 86 (F. '96).

Sullivan, Sir Arthur. Dub. Univ. 94: 485. (K. Field) Scrib. 18: 904.

(**Stockton,** John D.) Charlotte Cushman. Scrib. 12: 262 (Je. '76).

(**Stoddard,** Alfred.) Sydney Armstrong. Lippinc. 51: 104 (Ja. '93).

Julia Marlowe. Lippinc. 48: 306.

E. S. Willard. Lippinc. 51: 768 (Je. '93).

(**Stoddard,** Chas. Warren.) Behind the Scenes. Atlan. 34: 527 (N. '84).

Drama in Honolulu. Overland n. s. 2: 118.

(**Stoker,** Bram.) Actor Management. 19th Cent. 26: 1040 (Je. '90).

Dramatic Criticism. No. Am. 158: 325 (Mr. '94).

Storms on the Stage. Ev. Sat. 13: 269.

(**Stoughton,** J.) William Shakspere. Leis. Hour 13: 215, 279.

"**Strafford.**" *See "Browning."*

(**Strobel,** A.) Comédie Française. Murray 6: 335. Same art. Ecl. M. 113: 552.

Strolling Players. *See "Players."*

(**St. John,** J. A.) Lady Macbeth. Ecl. M. 16: 202.

(**Street**, J. M.) "Coriolanus." N. Eng. M. 51 : 260.

(**Stuart**, C.) Clara Morris. The. '81, 1 : 145.

(**Stuart**, Wm.) John S. Clarke. Lippinc. 18 : 497.

(**Sturgess**, Beatrice.) Some Famous Juliets. Peterson n. s. 6 : 1065 (O. '96).

Sturgis, Julian. Comedies. Spec. 55 : 445. Spec. 55 : 960. Sat. R. 53 : 675.

(**Sturgis**, J. R.) Shaksperian Revivals in London. Internat. R. 6 : 650.

(**Stutzer**, A.) Theatre in Germany. Belgra. 6 : 476; 28 : 476.

Subsidized Theatres. *See* "*National Theatre*," *etc.*

Suburban Theatres. (H. Elliott) The. n. s. 26 : 273 (N. '95).

Success on the Stage. (J. McCullough, J. Jefferson, Maggie Mitchell, Modjeska, L. Barrett, Wm. Warren) No. Am. (Je. '90).

Sudermann, Hermann. (Miss Braddon) National 21 : 751 (Ag. '93).
"Die Ehre." Quart. 182 : 399 (O. '95). (Miss Braddon) The. n. s. 25 : 131 (Mr. '95).
"Heimath." Quart. 142 : 399 (O. '95).

Sullivan, Sir Arthur. (K. Field) Scrib. 18: 904. *See also* "*Gilbert and Sullivan.*"

(**Sullivan**, M. F.) Origin of the Drama. Month 50: 554.

"**Supe**," Amateur, Story of an. (R. Keeler) Atlan. 32: 77.

"**Supers**" at the Theatre. All the Year 27: 438.

Supernumeraries, Gentlemen, in Canada. The. n. s. 26 : 277 (N. '95).

Swedish Drama. For. Quar. R. 2 : 208. Lippinc. 15 : 123 (Ja. '75). *See* "*Norwegian Drama.*"

Sweden, Drama in. The. n. s. 27 : 340 (Ja. '96).

Swordsmanship, Stage. (W. H. Pollock) The. n. s. 27 : 321 (Je. '96).

Taber, Julia Marlowe, Mrs.   (A. Stoddart) Lippinc. 48 : 306.
(B. Fletcher) Godey 132 : 589 (Je. '96).
as Rosalind.   Poet Lore 1 : 141 (Mr. '89).

Tableaux, A Chapter on.   Scribner : (N. '80).

(Talbot, F.)   Trades and Crafts of Shakspere.   Belgra. 26 :
49.

Talent and Genius on the Stage.   (G. Barlow) Contemp. 62 :
385 (D. '92).

(Talfourd, T. N.)   Hazlitt's Lectures on the Drama.   Ed. R.
34 : 438.

Talfourd, T. Noon. Athenian Captive : a Tragedy. Ed. R. 68 :
181. Mod. R. 146 : 173. Dub. R. 5 : 224.
Ion : a Tragedy. Quart. 54 : 505. Ed. R. 63 : 143.
Blackw. 126 : 419. (C. C. Felton) No. Am. 44 : 485.
(T. D. Woolsey) Chr. Q. Spec. 10 : 156. Fraser 14 :
218. Colburn 47 : 342. So. Lit. J. 4 : 289. (E. A.
Meredith) Canad. Mo. 8 : 38.

Talma, François Joseph, and the Dramatic Art.   (E. A.
Mathieu) The. '83, 1 : 265. Blackw. 18 : 297. All the
Year 40 : 183. Temp. Bar. 47 : 27. Same art. Ecl. M.
87 : 205. Dub. Univ. 48 : 704. Same art. Ecl. M. 40 :
216.   Colburn 5 : 12 ; 56 : 15 ; 72 : 536.
As an Actor.   Ev. Sat. 10 : 334.

"Taming of the Shrew." Harper 75 : 152 (Je. '87). (F. A.
Marshall and P. Fitzgerald) The. n. s. 12 : 10.   Temp.
Bar. 35 : 539. All the Year 44 : 511. (D. J. Snider)
Western 2 : 321. (Mrs. A. Gowing) The. n. s. 11 :
188. (A. Lang) Harper 90 : 89 (D. '94).

(Tawse, G.)   First Appearance of Mrs. Kendal in London.
The. n. s. 11 : 33.

(Taylor, T.)   Shortcomings of English Theatre.   Dark Blue
1 : 746.
English Stage.   Ev. Sat. 7 : 193.

(Taylor, W. M.)   The Essentials of Eloquence.   Princ. 3 :
177.

"**Tempest.**" (A. Lang) Harper 84 : 653 (Ap. '92). (F.
    A. March) Nation 55 : 112 (Ag. 11, '92).
    Burnand's Burlesque on. Sat. R. 56 : 275.
    Miranda and Ferdinand, Caliban and Ariel (W. J.
    Rolfe) Poet Lore 3 : 190.
    Montague on. Sat. R. 55 : 590.
    On the Stage. (A. Brereton) The. n. s. 10 : 59.

(**Ten Brock**, A.) Passion Play at Ober Ammergau. Hours
    at Home 3 : 527.

Tendencies of Shakspere. All the Year 46 : 38. Same art.
    Appleton 25 : 144.

Tennyson, Lord Alfred. Ed. R. 145 : 383.
    " Becket." Ath. '85, 1 : 7. Sat. R. 58 : 757 ; 75 : 145 (F.
       '93). Spec. 57 : 1699. Blackw. 138 : 57. Ecl. M. 105 :
       418. Macmil. 51 : 287 (F. '85). (M. F. Egan) Cath. W.
       42 : 382. (J. W. Mackail) Acad. 26 : 421. (F. Hawkins)
       The. '85, 1 : 53. (C. Nicholson) The Month 35 : 309.
    " Becket " at the Lyceum. Spec. 70 : 253 (F. '25,
       '93). (F. Wedmore) Acad. 43 : 158 (F. 18, '93). (J.
       Hatton) Art J. 45 : 105 (Ap. '93).
    " The Cup " and " The Falcon." Spec. 57 : 316. Ath.
       '84, 1 : 310. Appleton 25 : 253. St. James' 48 : 195.
    " Promise of May." Sat. R. 54 : 670. Spec. 55 : 1474.
       (F. Wedmore) Acad. 22 : 370. Harper 66 : 269 (F. '83).
    " Queen Mary." Quart. 139 : 231 (Jl.'75).
    Greek Drama vs. French. 19th Cent. 7 : 58.
    " Harold." (H. James, Jr.) Nation 24 : 43. (G. Bloede)
       Western 3 : 430. Chr. Obs. 77 : 308.

Terriss, William. The. '82, 2 : 332 ; '83, 1 : 329 ; n. s. 25 : 224
    (Ap. '95).
    as Romeo. The. '85, 1 : 16.
    Ellaline. The. n. s. 23 : 130 (Mr. '94).

Terry, Edward. The. n. s. 19 : 47 (Ja. '92).

Terry, Ellen. The. '78, 2 : 1, 15 ; '83, 2 : 30. (D. Cook)
    The. '80, 1 : 340. The. n. s. 25 : 160 (Mr. '95). (E.
    M. McKenna) McClure 2 : 457 (Ap. '94).

Terry, Ellen, as Beatrice. (W. D. Adams) The. '80, 2 : 216.
as Portia. The. '80, 1 : 49.
as Queen Catharine. The. n. s. 19 : 101 (F. '92).
Bernhardt, Duse, and. (Maud Andrews) New Bohemian
2 : 184 (My. '96).
Irving and. Harper 69 : 303 (Ag. '84). *See also " Irving."*

Terry, Fred. Mr. and Mrs. (Julia Neilson). The. n. s. 24 :
102, 118 (S. '94). (W. A. L. Bettany) The. n. s. 19 :
109 (S. '92).

Terry, Marion. The. '78, 2 : 267; '83, 1 : 94; n. s. 25 : 197
(Ap. '95).
as Mrs. Erlyne. The. n. s. 19 : 201 (Ap. '92).

Tercentenary of Shakspere. (M. D. Conway) Harper 29 :
337. N. E. Reg. 18 : 319. Brit. Quar. R. 29 : 253.

Text of Shakspere. (R. G. White) Atlan. 8 : 257. So. Lit.
Mess. 3 : 761.
Improvements in. (J. W. (Cole) Calcraft) Dub. Univ. 41 :
356.

(Tetley, A.) Humor of Molière. Macmil. 56 : 190.

Thackeray, Wm. M., and the Theater. (D. Cook) Longm.
4 : 409. Same art. Critic 5 : 80, 92.
Dramatic Adaptation of Works of. (C. P. Johnson)
Ath. 2 : 107, 171 (Jl. and Ag. '92).

Theater, an American Endowed. (Fredk. Ives Carpenter) :
Dial (Ch.) 21 (O. 1, '96).
Architecture of. (E. A. E. Woodrow.) Am. Arch. 44 : 18,
59, 119; 45 : 35, 71; 46 : 24, 124 (Ap.–D.'94).
Author and. (Geo. P. Lathrop) Dr. Mirror 24 : 600 (Je.
28, '90).
Buildings. (J. Hollingshead) The. n. s. 28 : 73 (Ag.
'96).
Building, Regulations for. Am. Arch. 36 : 38, 103; 38 :
22, 118 (Ap. 16 and My. 4, '92).

23

(**Thornbury**, W.)   London Theatres and Actors.   Belgra. 7 :
    360, 546; 8 : 70, 230, 394 ; 10 : 104, 248, 512.
(**Thoms**, W. J.)   German Drama and Early English.   Col-
    burn 61 : 19.
(**Thorpe**, Otway.)   Juliet.   The. n. s. 22 : 253 (N. '93).
(**Thorpe**, Winton.)   Peculiarity of French Stage.   The. n. s.
    24 : 51 (Ag. '94).
Tilbury, Zeffie, in "Ruth's Romance."   The. '85, 1 : 247,
    260.
"**Titus Andronicus.**"   Knowl. 11 : 99.   (F. Robinson)
    Contemp. 65 : 392 (Mr. '94).   Same art Ecl. M. 121 :
    547 (Ap. '94).   Also Liv. Age 201, 233 (Ap. '94).
    (R. G. Latham) Fraser 82 : 361.
(**Todd**, C. B.)   Fanny Kemble at Lennox.   Lippinc. 52 : 66
    (Jl. '93).
Toilers of the Stage.   (Alphonse Daudet) The. n. s. 24 :
    1 (Jl. '94).
(**Tolman**, A. H.)   Studies in Macbeth.   Atlan. 69 : 241 (F.
    '92).
(**Tompkins**, I. G.)   Women of Shakspere.   Chaut. 16 : 74
    (O. '92).
Toole, John Lawrence.   The. '79, 2 : 151.   The. '80, 1 : 317.
    Once a Week, 26 : 233.   Tinsley, 14 : 221.   Ev. Sat.
    15 : 442.   (J. Knight) The. '80, 1 : 24.
    Reminiscences.   Spec. 68 : 782 (Je. 4, '92).
    Humor, New, and Non-Humorists.   National 21 : 449
    (Je. '73).
(**Towle**, G. M.)   G. H. Lewes.   Appleton 5 : 133.
(**Townsend**, H.)   American Theatres.   Am. Arch. 35 : 28
    (Ja. 9, '92).
(**Townsend**, W.)   Clown in "Twelfth Night."   Canad. Mo. 4 :
    59 (N. '94).
(**Towse**, J. Rankin.)   Edwin Booth.   Nation 56 : 434 (Je. 13,
    '93).
    Eleanora Duse.   Cent. 51 : 130 (N. '95).
    John Gilbert.   Cent. 13 : 378.

(**Tree,** Herbert Beerbohm.) on Henrik Ibsen. Gent. M. n. s.
48: 103 (Ja. '92).

Should Dramatic Critics Write Plays? The. n. s. 26: 317
(D. '95).

The Production of Literary Plays. Fortn. 54: 925.

Tree, Mr. and Mrs., at the Haymarket. (W. A. L. Bettany)
The. 23: 75 (F. '94).

Tree, Mrs. Beerbohm. The. n. s. 28: 59 (Ag. '96).

Tree's Monday Nights of Literary Plays, Mr. Fortn. 54: 925.

Tricks of the Trade. (Mrs. Minnie Maddern Fiske) Dr.
Mirror 23: 589 (Ap. 12, '90).

"**Trilby.**" *See " George Du Maurier."*

(**Trollope,** A.) George II. Lewes. Fortn. 31: 15. Same art.
Liv. Age 140: 307.

(**Trollope,** H. M.) French Drama. Macmil. 31: 522.
J. B. P. Molière. Fraser 169: 273.
Molière, Début on the Stage. Blackw. 150: 486.
" Le Misanthrope." Gent. M. n. s. 40: 192.
"Tartufe." Blackw. 154: 641 (N. '93).

(**Trumbull,** Jonathan.) Walt Whitman's View of Shakspere.
Poet Lore 2: 368 (Jl. '90).

(**Trux,** J. J.) Negro Minstrelsy. Putnam 5: 73.

Turner, Chas. T. (A. B. Grosart) Leis. Hour 24: 711.

(**Turner,** Godfrey.) Amusement of the English People. 19th
Cent. 2: 820 (D. '77).
Dickens and the Play. The. '85, 1: 171.
Falstaff's Letters. The. '85, 2: 291.
Pantomime Clowns. The. '84, 1: 194.
Theaters of London. The. n. s. 14: 65.

(**Turner,** H.) Recollections of John Ryder. The. '85, 1: 222.

(**Tweedie,** Mrs. Alex.) Björnsen and Ibsen. Temp. Bar 98:
536 (Ag. '93).

(**Twiss,** H.) Mrs. Charles Mathews. Bentley 22: 93.

"Two Gentlemen of Verona." (D. J. Snider) J. Spec. Philos.
   10: 194. (A. M. Lethe) Acad. (Syr.) 7: 24 (F. '92).

(Tyrwhitt, R. St. J.) Passion Play and Symbolic Christianity.
   Contemp. 18: 234.

(Upson, A. J.) Frances Anne Kemble in America. Critic
   22: 152 (Mr. 11, '93).

Vanbrugh, Violet. The. n. s. 25: 5 (Ja. '95).

(Van de Velde, Mme.) Alex. Dumas, *fils*. Fortn. (Ja. '96):

(Vandam, A. D.) Comédie Française of To-Day. New
   R. 9: 314 (S. '93).
   Adaptation. Tinsley 19: 499.

(Van Rensselaer, W. G.) Sarah Bernhardt. Lippinc. 27:
   180 (F. '81).

(Venables, Gilbert.) Ophelia's Madness. National 4: 853
   (F. '85).

(Venning, K.) Emotional Acting in Paris. The. n. s. 10:
   240.
   Bernhardt as La Tosca. The. n. s. 11: 46; 12: 97. The.
   20: 46: 21: 97. Critic 18: 85.
   Dramatic Criticism in Paris. The. n. s. 10: 193.

Vestris, Marie Auguste. (T. P. Grinstead) Bentley 40: 255.
   Same art. Ecl. M. 39: 346.

Voice, Culture of. Atlan. 63: 568. *See Elocution,"* etc.
   American Conversational. Why it is Bad. (F. Osgood)
   Forum 19: 501 (Je. '95).
   Training of. Atlan. 62: 715.

Vanderfelt, E. H., as Judah. The. n. s. 19: 152 (Mr.
   '92).

Vaughan, Kate. (K. Hollingshead) The. n. s. 27: 257 (My.
   '96).

(Verney, Lady F. P.) Mysteries and Moralities. Contemp.
   25: 595.

Ventilation of New Paris Theatres.   (A. Morin) J. Frank. Inst. 76 : 369.

Ventilating, Warming, and Fire-Proofing of Theatres.   J. Frank. Inst. 76 : 170.

Wagner as a Dramatist.   (E. Rose) Fraser (99 : 519).

(Wagner, Leopold.)   Dramatic Illusion.   The. n. s. 26 : 87 (Ag. '95).

    Playwriting, Past and Present.   The. n. s. 28 : 66 (Ag. '96).

(Waldstein, Chas. D.)   Court Theatre of Meiningen.   Harper 82 : 743.

(Walker, Dr.)   Autobiography of Mrs. Anna Cora Mowatt Ritchie.   Howitt 3 : 146, 168, 181.

    Tendencies of the Stage.   Evang. R. 8 : 564.

(Walkley, A. B.)   English Drama.   Cosmopolis 1 : 88 (Ja. '96).

    Maid Marian on the Stage.   The. n. s. 19 : 277 (My.'92).

    Some Plays of the Day.   Fortn. 59 : 468 (Ap. '93).

    Theatres in London.   Cosmopolis 4 : 74 (O. '96).

    The Public as Fetish.   The. n. s. 24 : 283 (D. '94).

(Wall, A. H.)   Actor-Managers.   Lond. Soc. 43 : 296.

(Wall, J. W.)   Rise and Progress of the Drama.   Knick. 44 : 59.

Wallack, Elliston and.   (J. H. Siddons) Harper 25 : 73 (Je. '62).

Wallack, J. W.   Harper 24 : 73.

(Wallack, Lester.)   Memories of the Last Fifty Years.   Scrib. 4 : 411, 582, 719 (O., N. and D. '88).

Waller, Lewis.   The. n. s. 24 : 248 (N. '94).   (W. A. L. Bettany) The. n. s. 20 : 109 (S. '92).

(Waller, W. F.)   Sardou's "Cléopatre."   The. '83, 1 : 85, 362, 378.

(Wallis, D.)   At the Music Hall.   Longm. 22 : 163 (Je. '93).

(**Watson**, Malcomb.) Charity Matinées. The. n. s. 27: 216
(Ap. '96).

Death of A. G. Reed and C. Green. The. n. s. 25: 221
(Ap. '95).

Mr. Grundy and the Critics. The. n. s. 24: 161 (O.'94).

Spanish Drama. The. n. s. 10: 127.

Turn of the Tide. The. n. s. 26: 134 (S. '95).

Webster, Benjamin. The. n. s. 20: 23 (Jl. '92). (J. P.
Simpson) The. '82, 2: 83. Acad. 22: 56.

Webster, Benjamin, 2d, Mr. and Mrs. The. n. s. 26: 191
(O. '95).

Wilde, Oscar. "Lady Windermere's Fan." Spec. 69: 767
(N. 6, '92).

Wildenbruch, von, Ernst. Poet Lore 3: 481 (S. '91).

(**Wedmore**, Frederick.) Mary Anderson in England. Acad.
24: 168.

Mary Anderson in " Pygmalion and Galatea." Acad. 24:
440.

"Becket" at the Lyceum. Acad. 43: 158 (F. 18, '93).

Ada Cavendish. Acad. 48: 302 (O. 12, '95).

"Claudian" on the Stage. Acad. 24: 404.

Obituary of Edw. Dutton Cook. Acad. 24: 404.

Revival of the Drama in London. 19th Cent. 13: 217.

"Jane Eyre" on the Stage. Acad. 23: 33.

"Fédora" on the Stage. Acad. 23: 336.

Henry Irving in " Romeo and Juliet." Acad. 21: 200.

" School for Scandal." Acad. 21: 109.

Irving's Macbeth. Acad. 35: 14.

"King Henry VIII." at the Lyceum. Eng. Illust. 9:
291 (Ja. '92).

W. S. Gilbert's " Ruddygore." Acad. 31: 118.

Zola and the Comédie Française. Gent. M. n. s. 23: 60.

(**Wedgwood**, J.) Midsummer Night's Dream. Contemp.
57: 580.

(**Weiss**, J.) The Stage and Nature. Putnam 14: 63.

(**Weigland**, M.) Interpretations of Ibsen. Dial (Ch.) 16:
262 (My. 1, '94).

(**Westbrook**, Raymond.) The Domestic Drama. Atlan. 41:
353 (Mr. '78).

Westminster Abbey, Actors and Actresses in. Cornh. 67:
373 (Ap. '93).

(**Wheatley**, H. B.) Story of " Romeo and Juliet." Antiq.
n. s. 5 : 250 ; 6 : 246.
"Measure for Measure." Antiq. n. s. 8 : 200.

(**Wheeler**, A. A.) " Macbeth " with Kelly's Music. Overland
n. s. 7 : 185.

(**Wheeler**, A. C.) Actresses Who Have Become Peeresses.
Cosmop. 20 : 130 (D. '95).
Dion Boucicault. Arena 3 : 47 (D. '90).
Extinction of Shakspere. Arena 1 : 423.

Wheeler, D. H. Lovers in Shakspere. Chaut. 15 : 558
(Ag. '92).

(**Whipple**, E. P.) The Genius of Shakspere. Atlan. 20 : 178.
Old English Dramatists. No. Am. 63 : 29.

(**White**, M., Jr.) Sarah Bernhardt. Munsey 14 : 323 (D.
'95).

(**White**, R. G.) Drama of the Period. Galaxy 8 : 678.
Fechter's Hamlet. Nation 10 : 118.
Fechter's Realism. Nation 10 : 364.
French Tragedy. Atlan. 47 : 827.
Hamlet. Galaxy 9 : 535.
King Lear. Atlan. 46 : 111 ; 48 : 824.
Sarah Bernhardt. Atlan. 47 : 95.
Stage Rosalinds. Atlan. 51 : 248.
T. Salvini. Nation 17 : 213.
Text of Shakspere. Atlan. 8 : 257.
The Art of Shakspere. Atlan. 3 : 657.
" The School for Scandal." Atlan. 52 : 566.

(**Whitman**, S.) German Drama. Chaut. 21 : 163 (My. '95).
24

"**Winter's Tale**," Mary Anderson in. *See* "*Mary Anderson*," *etc.*

(W. Archer) The. n. s. 10: 214. Acad. 41: 18 (Ja. 2, '92). (A. Lang) Harper 88: 710 (Ap. '94). All the Year 41: 321. (D. J. Snider) J. Spec. Philos. 9: 80.

Stage History of. (W. Archer) 19th Cent. 12: 511.

(**Wills**, W. G.) Dramatic License. The. '80, 1: 199.

(**Winter**, Wm.) The Actor and his Duty to his Time. The. 23: 134.

Edwin Booth. Harper 63: 61 (Je. 81).

Henry Irving. The. '84, 2: 43, 86.

Joseph Jefferson. Harper 73: 391 (Ag. '86).

The Jeffersons. Cent. 2: 468.

Moral Influence of the Drama. No. Am. 136: 581.

(**Winton**, A.) W. S. Gilbert. The. n. s. 14: 71.

(**Withrow**, W. H.) Early English Drama. Meth. R. 54: 534.

Woffington, Margaret. Dub. Univ. 64: 180. (F. P. Cobbe) St. James' 43: 807.

Daly's Tribute to "Peg." Sat. R. 65: 671.

and G. A. Bellamy, Rival Actresses. Temp. Bar 52: 316.

Career of. (D. Cook) Once a Week 9: 61.

Margaret ("Peg"). Sat. R. 58: 605.

Recollections of. Colburn 52: 383.

Woman in Comedy. (C. T. Congdon) Harper 37: 507 (S. '68).

Woman Characters of Molière. Pub. Opin. 21: 63 (N. 12, '96).

Women Dramatists. English Dom. M. 11: 27.

Women and Amateur Acting. (F. A. Matthews) No. Am. 159: 759 (D. '94).

as Dramatists. All the Year 75: 296 (S. 29, '94).

as Writers of Female Comedy. (H. Elliott) The. n. s. 27: 328 (Je. '96).

(Wurtzburg, C. A.) "Much Ado About Nothing." Dramatic
　　Passion in. Poet Lore 6 : 550 (N. '94).
　　" Much Ado About Nothing," Introduction to. Poet
　　　Lore 6 : 70 (F. '94).

Wyndham, Charles, as Charles Surface. The. n. s. 17 : 253.
　　as David Garrick. (W. Calvert) The. n. s. 18 : 9 ; 27 :
　　　194 (Ap. '96).
　　in " London Assurance." The n. s. 17 : 41.
　　in " She Stoops to Conquer." The n. s. 15 : 311.
　　as Bob Sacket. The. n. s. 19 : 50 (Ja. '92).
　　as Peregrine Porter. The n. s. 19 : 153 (Mr. '92).

(Wyndham, Charles.) Actor Management. 19th Cent. 26 :
　　1040 (Je. '90).
　　Tendencies of Modern Comedy. No. Am. 149: 607
　　　(D. '87).

(Yates, E.) At the Play. Temp. Bar 19 : 476.

Yohe, May. The. n. s. 23 : 26 (Ja. '94) ; 26 : 255 (N. '95).

(Young, J. C.) Charles Mathews. Canad. Mo. 2 : 183, 274.

Young, Sir Charles. " Linda Grey." The. n. s. 17 : 254.

(Young, Sir Charles.) The Drama. Once a Week 26 : 318
　　348.

(Zimmern, H.) T. Salvini on Shakspere. Gent. M. n. s.
　　32 : 131.

Zola, Emile. Attack on Modern Drama. (M. Hapgood) Harv.
　　Mo. 9 : 160.

Zola and the Comédie Française. (F. Wedmore) Gent. M. n.
　　s. 23 : 60.

www.ingramcontent.com/pod-product-compliance
Lightning Source LLC
Chambersburg PA
CBHW030539040726
47497CB00008B/2516

* 9 7 8 3 3 3 7 3 0 6 0 7 6 *